Desert Blossom

Rebecca Grace

A Wings ePress, Inc.
Contemporary Romance Novel

Wings ePress, Inc.

Edited by: Lorraine Stephens
Copy Edited by: Sara Reinke
Senior Editor: Anita York
Executive Editor: Lorraine Stephens
Cover Artist: Trisha Fitzgerald-Petri

All rights reserved

Names, characters and incidents depicted in this book are products of the author's imagination or are used fictitiously. Any resemblance to actual events, locales, organizations, or persons, living or dead, is entirely coincidental and beyond the intent of the author or the publisher.

No part of this book may be reproduced or transmitted in any form or by any means, electronic or mechanical, including photocopying, recording, or by any information storage and retrieval system, without permission in writing from the publisher.

Wings ePress Books
www.wingsepress.com

Copyright © 20xx by
ISBN 13: 978-1-59088-560-4

Published In the United States Of America

Wings ePress Inc.
3000 N. Rock Road
Newton, KS 67114

Reviewers Praise Rebecca's First Wings Novel Love On Deck

"...a book not to be missed. LOVE ON DECK is a fun and exciting read... This is the first romance Rebecca Martinez has written with Wings ePress and with her refreshing story line and incredible writing ability, she is sure to go far." —4 Blue Ribbons

—Dina Smith,
Romance Junkies.com

"LOVE ON DECK is a modern story where the characters come alive with the believable interplay and dialogue... This very original story will captive readers with its consistent characters and well developed plot." --4 ½

—Amelia Richards,
Cataromance Reviews

Though I am not a huge baseball fan—football is more my thing—Rebecca Martinez bats contemporary romance out of the park in her new one, LOVE ON DECK... 4 Roses

—Shannon
romancereaderatheart.com

Dedication

To Ron,
who gave me back my writing dream
and made this story possible.

* * *

One

"I hate Las Vegas when I lose. How are you doing?" Billie Rogers asked in a bored voice, tapping cigarette ashes into an empty drink glass beside her slot machine.

Maggie Hemple wrinkled her nose as three cherries popped up on the screen of her machine. Her credits went up by three. Not bad, except she had bet five nickels. "Not so well. I haven't done any milking in a while."

"Me, either. I'm about finished. How about you?"

"Almost."

Checking her watch, Billie hit the spin button one final time. She muttered a curse and sighed. "I should round up Jack. We have to hurry if we're going to make the ninety-nine-cent breakfast special at Dusty's. I'm not paying three dollars when I can get it for a buck if we get there before seven. We'd better start thinking about hitting the road if we want to get home by noon."

Maggie hit the button to spin. She was used to her friend's impatience. The two had known each other since grade school, though they hadn't become close until seven years ago when they began working together after Billie's divorce. This trip to Las Vegas was Billie's birthday gift to Maggie--not that it was such an extravagant gift. The hotel room cost twenty dollars a night, and for meals they'd been dining on cheap buffets, low-priced steaks and the ninety-nine-cent breakfast special.

As the weekend wound down, Maggie sat at a video machine called "Rags to Riches." She'd dubbed it "The Milking Game." Among the apples, oranges and cherries were farm animals. Get more than three cows on the screen and she got to milk one for a jackpot. Select the right cow and bells went off as the bucket overflowed with coins. Get the wrong one, and the cow might give only one coin, accompanied by a sickly moo.

She had discovered the game their first night in town and had been playing regularly ever since. Maggie pushed her thick glasses up her nose and shoved a wayward lock of hair behind one ear. Beside her, Billie stood on one foot, her other knee resting on the vinyl seat. Her neck craned as she peered around the casino.

Following her gaze, Maggie surveyed the casino. She saw no sign of Jack's tall figure. The cavernous room dripped gaudiness from the overdone chandeliers to the bright red and gold carpet. The sound of jingling coins and the monotonous drone of slot machine sound effects filled the air. Lights blinked everywhere, either advertising winners or promising high pay offs. The small crowd was like an ocean tide-- ebbing and then rushing forward with renewed vigor, but always on the move. Cocktail waitresses in skimpy skirts and halter tops offered drinks in husky voices despite the early hour. A thin layer of smoke hung in the stale morning air. Maybe he'd gone outside to escape the smoke. Or to get away from her and Billie.

A cigarette hung from Billie's thin lips. She tossed back her thick red hair and took a deep drag of the cigarette, letting the smoke swirl around her head. Luckily for her, Las Vegas was possibly the last place anyone would ever enact a smoking ordinance.

"I can't believe Jack keeps disappearing like this," she said in disgust, flicking her ashes into a plastic cup this time. "Why did he come if he's going to spend all his time wandering around instead of gambling? I don't think he's put more than a couple of fives into the machines."

Maggie made no comment. Jack was her neighbor, and she had issued the invitation, though she wasn't certain why he had come. He didn't seem to enjoy gambling and now there was no telling where he was. All three had risen at five after a long night of visiting casino after casino along the Strip. The two women had wanted to get in a final round of gambling, but as he'd been doing since they'd arrived, Jack had said he preferred to walk around.

She had no idea where he went or what he was doing. He knew they needed to get home by noon. Maggie and Billie had arranged their schedules so they didn't have to be at work until then. That left time for breakfast before the two-hour drive through the desert to their hometown of Cactus Bluffs.

Maggie cast a quick glance at her watch. Quarter to seven. Right now her twin girls, April and May should be getting out of bed and getting ready for school. Maggie made a mental note to call them before breakfast to make certain their babysitter hadn't let them oversleep.

The points in her machine flashed up at her. Seventy-five nickels left. She was playing five coins every time she pushed the button.

"You might as well see if you can find Jack. I'll be done by the time you get back."

"Make it quick," Billie admonished with another meaningful glance at her watch. "It's not often you get ham and eggs for ninety-nine cents."

"Okay," Maggie agreed. "This machine is strange. It pays a little, then a lot and then goes for a long period without paying much at all."

"Play maximum coins. It can't hurt. I'm hungry and I'm not facing that long drive through the desert without breakfast."

Maggie smiled up at her friend and patted her ample hip. "Hey, you need it. I could stand to miss a few meals." It never ceased to amaze her how her thin friend could eat anything she wanted and not gain an ounce, while Maggie had to watch every calorie. Despite the constant dieting, she still needed to lose at least thirty pounds. "Let me just finish this up."

She knew better than to argue with Billie when hunger was the issue. She punched the line for the maximum of twenty-five coins and watched her credits slip to fifty as the machine began to spin. The lines flew up. Nothing. She hit the button again. Another spin. Another screen full of disconnected images. No cows.

"Okay," she said unhappily. "Final spin." She punched the button, and the machine spun again. One black and then one white cow came up on the screen. That was followed by a third, which drew a little cry from Maggie.

"Hey, I get to milk!" she said in delight, pointing at the machine as she turned toward her friend.

Billie was gone, having disappeared around the row of tall machines. Maggie's unruly curls flopped in her face, and she pushed them back behind her ear again She was on her own.

She held her hand poised over the buttons, then gulped. A fourth cow had come up on the screen. To her amazement, a fifth cow appeared and stopped on the line.

"Oh, my gosh," she squealed, looking around desperately for Billie. "Oh, my gosh."

Jack's tall, lanky figure appeared out of nowhere, large hands shoved in the pockets of his jeans.

"How are you doing?" he asked, stopping in front of her.

Maggie jumped up from the machine and hurled herself at him, throwing her arms around him and hugging him. "Five cows!" she cried. "Five cows!"

She hopped up and down as the machine began to play "Old MacDonald" and the screen changed. Her hair flew wildly around her face, but this time she didn't care. A barn appeared and five video cows with silly expressions took over the screen. The song faded and the sound of mooing emitted from the machine. Maggie's fingers shook and she gripped Jack's hand without thinking.

"I can't believe it!" she squealed.

"Hey, calm down," he said with a laugh, freeing his squeezed hand.

"I've never had five cows," she cried, excitement buzzing inside her. Her knees felt weak and she knelt on the seat. Maggie surveyed the machine and drew a mental blank as her fingers danced over the buttons under each cow. "Oh, my gosh! Which one should I pick? Which one?"

"Hell if I know," Jack said and flicked a long finger at a black and white Hereford named Betsy. Maggie pushed the button below Betsy and the bucket began to fill--and continued filling with coins until it overflowed. The machine began to sing "Old MacDonald" again in a louder tone, and the sound of a whole herd of cows mooing filled the air.

"I got the big jackpot!" she exclaimed in an unbelieving tone as the machine flashed the final coin amount.

"Wow," Jack said leaning over to pat her shoulders.

Maggie whirled around and hugged his tall frame without thinking. "You did it!" she cried. "You picked my winning cow!" This time as she separated from Jack, his gaze met hers and a strange electric current raced though her.

Had she ever noticed how blue his eyes were? Why had she never noticed how tall he was--she barely came halfway up his chest. A hard, wide chest at that. How had she missed seeing that his lean cheek creased with a dimple when he smiled or how his eyes crinkled with little laugh lines at the corners? Had she ever realized how very black his hair was, short and crisply cut? And what about that crooked grin that promised mischief? Had she ever really noticed him before?

She shook off the sudden bout of physical awareness. It was the win, Maggie told herself. The excitement of the jackpot that had her suddenly aware of Jack. He was just her neighbor.

His boyish smile beamed approval at her. "You're a real winner," he said with an exaggerated wink.

Her breath was coming faster than normal, but she wasn't so certain it had anything to do with the win. She looked around for Billie but saw no sign of her. The machine was singing out now and flashing like a police car trying to slow down a speeding driver.

Billie appeared around the row of machines, a scowl on her face. When she saw Jack, her thin lips pressed together in a frown of disapproval and then she took notice of the ringing machine with its flashing lights. Billie's eyes grew wide as she looked beyond her friend.

"You hit it?" she said in disbelief.

Maggie collapsed onto the hard seat, giggling wildly. "Yes, yes, yes!"

Billie screeched so loudly that nearby casino patrons turned to check out the ruckus.

Confusion reigned for the next few minutes as the floor manager came over to check on the ringing. He needed to verify the machine before he could pay her the jackpot of twenty-five hundred dollars. Billie and Maggie alternately giggled and hugged as they waited for the payoff. Jack kept patting her shoulder and calling her a winner. Maggie certainly felt like it.

The ninety-nine-cent breakfast special was forgotten as the trio became the center of attention on the casino floor. The machine kept ringing, and around them, a crowd of early gamblers gathered to find out what the jackpot paid. Finally the manager counted out twenty-five crisp one-hundred-dollar bills, and they left the casino.

Jack shoved his hands into his jean pockets as they walked out the door. The two women couldn't stop giggling. They sounded like Maggie's twin teenage daughters. He found he couldn't take his eyes off his neighbor. He had lived next to her for four years, but until this morning he'd never realized what an appealing woman she was.

Even behind the thick glasses, her brown eyes had danced in a lively fashion when she'd won the jackpot. And when she'd hugged him--not once, but twice--his body had reacted with a male awareness he hadn't felt with anyone for a long time. The roundness of her curves, the softness of her skin, the silky hair that teased his chin as she jumped, the faint clean scent of something floral all added up to a womanly package that was a pleasant surprise.

They stepped outside the casino into blistering sunlight. A hot, dry gust of wind sent dust and paper flying across the sidewalk. It might be eight in the morning, but the temperature was already baking the city.

"I'm still hungry," Billie grumbled. "Damn, we missed the ninety-nine-cent special."

"Don't worry about it. We can go any place we want," Maggie assured her with a giggle, waving her winnings.

"Okay, but you can buy," Billie teased as they walked toward Jack's SUV. She grabbed Maggie's hand and shoved it down. "Put that away before we get mugged! Jack doesn't want to have to fight off muggers this early in the morning."

"If I have to fight off anyone it won't be because of the money," Jack heard himself say, much to his surprise. "It will be because I'm with two of the prettiest girls in town."

Maggie's face turned bright pink and he couldn't resist the opportunity to wink at her.

"Jack, you old smoothie," Billie chided, tapping his arm playfully and then pulling out a fresh cigarette.

He and Billie had developed a teasing, jovial relationship over the few years he'd known her. Maggie had tried to set them up when he'd first moved in next door, but he had not been in the market for dating, and they'd quickly discovered they had little in common. Back in those days, he'd wondered why Maggie had showed no interest in him. In most places he'd lived, when single women had discovered he had no wife, they had made a play for him.

It had taken little time to discover why that hadn't happen with his neighbor. Maggie was waiting for her Prince Charming to return. He couldn't remember the name of the guy; he just knew what her twin daughters told him. Maggie expected their father to come back one day. From what he had seen of his neighbor in the past four years, she remained true to that ghost.

"Where shall we go?" Billie asked, looking up and down the block of hotel-after-gaudy- themed-hotel.

"Let's go some place special. And I get to pay," Jack announced. "As my thanks for bringing me."

Maggie shook her head, amber colored curls dancing around her head. "Jack, we can't do that. You already bought the gas and drove your car."

"I've been having fun. I've never been to Las Vegas before."

The gambling mecca had never drawn him, and while some of the men from the Air Force base where he was stationed were constantly inviting him on weekend trips, he'd never been tempted. Drunken gambling binges didn't sound appealing. Coming with Maggie and Billie had been different--he'd known he would be on his own to explore at his own pace. While the women had sat at slot machines, he'd wandered through the ostentatious hotels with their outlandish, garish casinos, watching the ever-moving crowd.

Much as he usually studied people, Jack found himself observing Maggie as they sat at breakfast feasting on bargain steak and eggs. He'd never really noticed how soft her skin looked, or how she could turn pink at the slightest hint of an off-color remark that Billie might toss her way.

"What are you going to do with your winnings?" Billie asked. "I think you should do something special for yourself."

Maggie's bright eyes grew large behind her thick glasses. He'd never noticed before but now they reminded him of a mug of root beer, sparkling and bubbly. Appealing.

"Well, the brakes need fixing on my car," she said.

"I can do that in a couple of hours if you get the parts," Jack volunteered, waving his fork. He hated to see her newly-won money thrown away on something he could easily fix, but her words didn't surprise him. Maggie was the sort of practical thinker who would immediately focus on importance rather than frivolity.

She blinked, those big eyes resting on him. A fork-speared piece of steak stopped halfway to her lips. Pink, full lips, he noticed.

"Jack, I couldn't ask that of you. You already do too much for us. I know that you've been helping the girls with the yard work and feeding Kayla when they conveniently forget."

He didn't mind the work. It kept him busy in his off hours. His own yard was the size of a postage stamp and never needed much care. Tending her grass gave him a chance to use his new set of garden tools.

"Let him do it," Billie urged, elbowing Maggie and winking at him. "It keeps him off the streets. Besides, you should spend that money on something other than giving it to rip-off artists who will charge you twice as much as necessary just because you're a woman."

Jack agreed. "Let me do the brakes. Spend the money on more personal things."

"The girls could use new clothes," Maggie admitted, smiling at him gratefully.

Her pink lips parted, displaying perfect, white teeth that sent another quick round of awareness through him. Why had he never noticed her before? And what good would it do to start now? Luckily, the women were too caught up in the magical winning moments to notice this crazy new world that seemed to be spinning around with him in it.

"A shopping expedition!" Billie cried with glee. "Let's go to Los Angeles next weekend."

"I should save some of the money," Maggie said, her smile lessening. "After all you never know when you might need it..."

"Oh, live a little," Billie urged. "Let's think of the most impractical thing we could do with that money. What would you do, Jack, if you had that much money?"

"Me?" He blinked, surprised at the sudden attention that was turned in his direction. He could feel Maggie's eyes on him, and he shifted uncomfortably. "I'm a poor subject to ask. I'd probably save it."

"Save it?" Billie hooted. "Not splurge on a wild weekend in Los Angeles with a couple of crazy blondes in a beachfront hotel room with a waterbed?"

Maggie turned pink, and Jack found his face growing warm. The thought didn't excite him. He probably would save the money. That was what he did with most of his paychecks. His small house didn't require much of an output, and his SUV was paid off.

"You're smart," Maggie said, nodding her head in approval in his direction. "It's good to think about the future."

"Oh, pooh, I'd splurge," Billie countered, thin lips drawing together into a line of disapproval as she looked from one to the other. "I'd buy me some swanky clothes and new CDs, maybe even a fancy new stereo system."

Jack had a new stereo system, and he hated to correct Billie and let her know the price for a good one went well beyond twenty-five-hundred dollars. She was urging Maggie to think of something extravagant, and as Maggie shrugged and fidgeted, he found himself wanting to hear what she might do if she splurged.

"Well, maybe I might spend a few days at the beach," he volunteered, hoping it would loosen her up and allow her to be more expressive. "Soaking up the sun."

"Now you're talking," Billie said. "What else? Watching the girls in their bikinis march up and down the boardwalk?"

He drummed his fingertips on the table top, feeling uncomfortable again and noted that Maggie was turning pink, a nice shade of pink, like bubblegum.

"Maybe," he said, forcing a nonchalant shrug. He was still curious about his neighbor. "What would you do with the money, Maggie, if you didn't have responsibilities? Be fanciful," he invited.

"Fanciful?" she repeated, blinking rapidly as though the thought was unimaginable. She pushed her glasses back up her small nose, and her brow furrowed. Her pink lips twisted into a familiar little pucker. "What would I do? I might take the girls--"

"No." Billie interrupted, hitting her arm playfully. "No girls. On your own."

Maggie turned toward Billie, eyes wide in surprise. "Go without the girls? I couldn't go anywhere... Oh." She clapped her hand to her lips. "I need to call them. Does anyone have a phone? I can't believe I didn't call them immediately and tell them about the prize."

Jack started to reach for his cell phone, but Billie had already produced hers out of a big straw bag. The phone call didn't surprise him. He'd witnessed Maggie's devotion to her twin daughters over and over. Now her face lit up as she began talking on the phone. He enjoyed watching her eyes gleam and her facial expressions grow animated as she told them about winning the jackpot.

She pushed her glasses up and he noted the scattering of freckles across her nose. Like so much about her today, he realized he'd never seen them before. He looked away. This was ridiculous. He couldn't be interested in her, could he? Then, as he turned his attention back to his eggs, he told himself no, even if he wanted to be, he wouldn't. She was still waiting for her girls' father to come back.

And he would never forget Carla. Just watching Maggie and having those strange thoughts made it seem like he was being untrue to Carla. Unbidden, a picture of his wife floated before his eyes, Carla of the long, flowing red hair, green eyes bright and luminous as emeralds, and movements so graceful that she seemed to be floating when she walked. Carla. Beautiful Carla. Jack shook his head to clear it of the vision before he dug back into his breakfast.

Maggie shut the phone and handed it back to Billie. Her eyes were wide and confused as she faced them. "They want a computer. Can you believe it? I offered clothes and CDs, and all they can talk about is getting a computer."

"Great idea," Billie said, tapping her on the shoulder. "I was wondering when you were going to join the new century."

The girls could make good use of a computer, but the thought disappointed him. Often April and May came over and borrowed his when they needed to complete a school project. He welcomed those moments of noise and disturbance in his otherwise quiet house.

"What would we do with a computer?" Maggie asked, shaking her head in bewilderment.

"There's a lot you can do," Billie said. "The girls can use it for school, and you wouldn't have to buy all those games for that Nintendo machine. And you could get on the internet. Go online. There's a lot of information on there."

"Right. You've told me over and over that all you do is flirt with guys online."

"You could, too," Billie said with a laugh, punching Maggie's arm again.

Maggie's eyes grew very large and surprised. "Why would I want to do that? I have plenty of men to flirt with from the Air Force Base, if I was that type. They come in all the time for gas and smokes, and they talk with you more than me, right, Jack?"

Jack chuckled and nodded in agreement. The pair worked as cashiers at a convenience store along the main road that cut through the desert town of Cactus Bluffs. The town was actually more of an intersection on the lonely freeway between Los Angeles and Las Vegas.

He was one of the men from the base who stopped in regularly. Maggie was friendlier, though Billie was quicker with a suggestive comment.

"Sure," Billie said. "But those guys keep getting younger and they only have one thing on their mind anyway."

Again that pinkish touch glowed on Maggie's cheeks. Jack watched the exchange with more interest than he wanted to admit, though he made no attempt to join in. He was curious about what Maggie might have to say about the lack of men in her life. The subject didn't come up often.

"I don't look at them that way," Maggie said, eyes cast down on the table.

"You don't look at all," Billie teased, jostling her friend playfully with a thin shoulder. "You have a big sign on your forehead that says, 'off limits, not interested.' This is different. You can meet men from all over the country, and just talk to them."

Maggie was shaking her head in dismissal, pink lips pressed together. "As long as I have my two girls, that's all I need."

"Those girls are growing up. They're already thirteen and getting minds of their own. They'll be dating soon," Billie warned.

Maggie wrinkled her nose. Jack knew how protective she was of the girls. They were two of the best-behaved teens he'd ever met.

"You need to do something to stir up your life," Billie continued. "You live your life for your girls."

"My girls are my life," she said quietly.

Jack could see she was growing uncomfortable. "That's not a bad plan for a mother to have," he offered. "More mothers should be that way."

Maggie sent him a wide, thankful smile that delivered a punch to his stomach so lethal, he nearly lost his breath. His body went rigid, and he picked up his coffee mug to hide his expression. Maggie! This wasn't good. He couldn't begin to see her as more than a neighbor. Could he?

Two

"Let's call in sick," Billie urged. "We can tell Dick we had car trouble. He doesn't know Jack drove. We'll say your car broke down and head over to LA and go shopping. We can be back by the time the girls get out of school."

The thought was tempting, but Maggie couldn't do that to Dick. He owned the convenience store, and if they didn't show up, he would end up working a double shift.

"We'd better not," Maggie said, wrinkling her nose. "Dick is depending on me to be there this afternoon, and I had to beg to get off this morning. I don't want to take advantage of him."

"Oh, all right. Sometimes you're just too damned honest."

Maggie laughed. "Not honest. Just good old, dependable Maggie Hemple. Besides we still have a couple of hours before we have to be at work."

Jack had dropped them off at Billie's and gone home. Maggie tried not to think of the crazy notions she'd had back in the casino as they'd said quick farewells. Billie had thanked him for driving with a hug, but Maggie had kept her distance. He would never look at her as anything more than his pudgy, often pesky, neighbor.

She slumped onto Billie's comfortable worn sofa and blew her hair off her face. It was only early May, but summer heat was already beginning to press into Cactus Bluffs. Before long the temperature would top one hundred degrees on a daily basis.

Billie brought her a glass filled with ice and soda, which Maggie gratefully accepted. They had laughed all the way back. Her winning the jackpot had made the trip across miles of barren desert more exciting. They'd taken turns detailing what they would do if they ever won one of the jackpots worth millions.

Travel was Billie's choice, while Maggie preferred the idea of assuring her daughters of a good college education and a nice home. Jack had surprised her. He wanted to open a chain of restaurants.

After flipping on a floor fan, Billie plopped down on a chair across from Maggie with her own glass.

"Still thinking about what to do with the money?" Billie asked.

"I'll spend it on the girls," Maggie said with a nod.

"You ought to use it to get out of this town," Billie said, taking a sip of her drink. "Your girls will be ready to get out of this place soon, and you need to think of yourself."

Maggie didn't like to think about her girls growing up. They were already making comments about leaving once they got old enough. She couldn't blame them. Cactus Bluffs was a desert hamlet that existed to serve the immediate needs of a nearby Air Force Base, once a prime location for pilot training. Even the Space Shuttle landed nearby at one time. Now, cutbacks had reduced the base to a repair and minor training facility.

Besides the Air Force presence, the town had little to recommend it. Filled with motels and restaurants, it provided a stopping point on a lonely desert road between Los Angeles and Las Vegas.

"You need to do something special with that money, Maggie," Billie urged. "Spice up your life."

A frown crossed Maggie's face. She looked beyond Billie to the bleak landscape outside. Beyond the street of small frame homes, the desert stretched, a barren wasteland. Brown clouds of dust blew across the street and down the block. Tumbleweeds tossed by the wind rested against a fence clogged with more weeds.

Sometimes Maggie worried that her life was as barren as the land around her. Yet when she and her girls were sitting around the kitchen table laughing, her life couldn't be happier.

"You won't always have those girls," Billie said, as though she knew what Maggie was thinking.

A moment of panic gripped Maggie. She couldn't fathom that. "Maybe they won't leave," she said quietly. Her parents still lived in Cactus Bluffs, though her two brothers and sisters had moved away years ago. Maggie often wondered why she stayed. At times she wanted to go. The dusty desert town held little for her, and often she feared she would never live down the mistakes of her past. And yet she stayed.

Billie stared at her soda glass thoughtfully, as though it was a crystal ball that held the answer. "They need to get out of here. We should all go."

"I don't see you in any rush to leave," Maggie pointed out and immediately regretted the catty sound of her voice. She and Billie talked about leaving from time to time, but most of it was wishful thinking.

Billie sighed heavily, a palm pounding the arm of her chair. "I guess you're right. We're stuck in this one-horse town, and we're too old to go anywhere."

"Maybe someday," Maggie said, taking a sip of her drink. "I could put some of this money aside and start saving to move."

"Buy a damn computer," Billie said forcefully, putting down her glass with such force that brown soda sloshed over the top. "We have time before work. Let me show you what it's all about."

~ * ~

"What is this?" Maggie asked breathlessly as she watched the blinking computer screen.

Billie sat in front of the keyboard and monitor on a rickety table. Maggie pulled up a chair beside her and watched over her shoulder as her friend tapped a couple of keys.

"Not much action on here during the morning," Billie grumbled, pulling out a cigarette.

Maggie adjusted her glasses and pushed them back up her sweating nose, focusing on the screen.

> *CNoah: 31/male/Florida.*
> *Witty1: 29/female, looking for the right guy.*
> *Lucky79: 21/m, looking for a female who likes to get wild...*
> *FunnyGuy: Hello room! Looks like my kind of place.*
> *JackeeO: Hi there. Could be.*
> *CNoah: Hi Witty. How will you know the right man?*
> *Witty1: Believe me, I'll know.*

"I don't understand," Maggie said, shaking her head in confusion. When she considered using a computer, she thought of playing video games or visiting websites for news and research.

"These people are chatting," Billie explained, waving her hand at the monitor. "This is called a chat room. You go there and talk to people from all over the country."

"They just talk?" Maggie asked, watching in amazement as the screen shifted with ongoing comments.

"Sure. You look for people who are interesting."

The conversation flowed by on the screen, a process that overwhelmed Maggie. She wasn't certain who was talking or answering even when Billie joined in using her screen name, Sweetie Pie.

> *WIZARD73: Hello. Any Ladies here like to chat?*
> *SweetiePie: I might! What do you have in mind, Wizard?*
> *CNoah: Hey, Sweetie, don't you want to talk to me?*
> *SweetiePie: I know you. I'm looking for new blood.*
> *CNoah: Thanks a bunch.*
> *Witty1: I'll talk to you, Noah.*

"You get on here," Billie said, getting up from the chair. "I'll get us another drink."

Maggie shook her head. "What do I do?"

"Just respond to what they're saying when you feel like it. Don't worry. They'll carry the conversation."

Drawing a deep breath, Maggie sat down at the keyboard. She had no idea what to say.

> *CNoah: Hey, Sweetie! Did you stop talking?*
> *Witty1: Maybe she doesn't like you.*
> *JackeeO: Who wants to talk to me? I'm a nice girl.*

Slowly Maggie began to type. By the time she wrote down a hello, and sent it, the others were discussing a different topic. Suddenly another box appeared on the top of the screen.

> *WIZARD73: Are you still there?*

She typed in an answer and hit send, but it appeared in the chat room.

> *SweetiePie: Yes.*
> *JackeeO: Yes, what, Sweetie?*

At the same time, another message appeared in the corner from Wizard, but she had no idea what to do with it. Billie reappeared with two fresh glasses of soda and handed her one.

"What's happening?" Billie asked, peering over her shoulder.

"Well, this guy is talking up here. But I don't know how to answer him." She pointed at the screen, frustration spilling out.

"Let me in there."

Billie took over control and Maggie watched. First Billie called up a page and typed in 'Wizard73.' A new full page flew up, and Billie read over it.

"What's that?"

"Profile. It tells me all about him. See? Thirty-four years old. Teacher from Ohio. Oh, he's single. Good." She lined up her mouse on the box where he had said hello and typed in a reply.

WIZARD73: Well, hello finally.

SweetiePie: I'm sorry. I ran to get something to drink.

WIZARD73: I was looking at your profile. Why aren't you married?

SweetiePie: Haven't found anyone I want to marry.

WIZARD73: Good answer.

SweetiePie: The truth. What about you? What's your reason?

WIZARD73: No Mrs. Right yet.

SweetiePie: No such critter as Mr. or Ms. Right.

WIZARD73: Maybe not. I like to think there is.

SweetiePie: A romantic. I haven't even found an almost.

WIZARD73: Where are the men in your life?

SweetiePie: Around, but I can always use another special guy.

"That's amazing," Maggie said, patting Billie on the shoulder. "Just like that, you're flirting with him."

"Sure, why not? It's kind of fun." Quickly she read over his reply and with a laugh, Billie typed out a clever response.

Maggie's eyes were wide as she looked at the screen. "This is unbelievable."

"Join the modern world, Mag. It's happening every day. People even meet on here and end up getting married."

"Unbelievable," she repeated.

Billie flashed a wicked smile and a wink. "I told you. This could be the answer to finding the man of your dreams."

Maggie stared at the comment about no such critter. She was like Wizard. She believed Mr. Right was out there. She even knew who it was. Al Williams. The father of her girls. The young Air Force man had won her heart when she had been seventeen. Al, with curly hair the color of straw and blue-green eyes that put the desert sky to shame. Al, with the shy smile and soft southern accent. Even now, she looked for him in every car that stopped for gas, in every blonde male customer who came into the store. Every time the bell chimed to announce someone entering, Maggie looked up, expecting Al to be returning as he'd once promised.

Maggie glanced at the computer where Billie still spoke to Wizard. Maybe the computer worked for some. She doubted it had much practical application for her.

~ * ~

Brilliant morning sunlight glistened on Jack's black hair as he jogged across the street toward his house next door. Maggie couldn't take her eyes off him as she watched from her kitchen window. His thighs churned, their hard lengths visible below dark shorts. The muscles of his arms rippled as they moved in a pumping motion. His black t-shirt clung to a wide, hard chest, the center stained dark by sweat. Virility screamed from him, but it had never made her catch her breath. Until now. Her breath was coming in shallow, quick spurts.

The voice behind her caught her attention, and she blinked as though waking up. She forced her attention from Jack returning from his normal morning run and turned around.

"Say that again." Maggie shoved a stray lock of hair behind her ear, staring in shock at her babysitter. Cassie Wilde slumped at the kitchen table, fanning herself with the check Maggie had just given her.

Outside, the desert wind had been howling since daybreak and promised a day of dust, though it didn't seem to affect Jack. The windows rattled and tumbleweeds blew across her small front lawn and caught on the fence. She moved away from the window, fearing Jack might see her watching him. Forcing her breath back into an even pace as the vision of Jack left her head, Maggie sat across from Cassie and tried to focus on her words.

"I'm getting married," Cassie said with a giggle, dropping the check on the table and tugging at a strand of washed-out, reddish hair.

The thought that Cassie was getting married was as shocking as the strange effect she'd had from seeing Jack exercise. It was a normal morning occurrence, but today she felt as short of breath as he probably was. Even her pulse had accelerated slightly.

"I didn't even know you were seeing anyone," Maggie said.

Like Maggie, Cassie had always lived in Cactus Bluffs. She was severely overweight, and the ravages of her teenage battle with acne still remained. She'd been Maggie's babysitter since the girls were toddlers. Though she was in her late twenties, Cassie still lived with her parents.

"You don't know him," Cassie said, cheeks growing pink and eyes lowering to the table as though she was embarrassed. "He's from Iowa."

"Are you certain about this? How well do you know him?"

Her discomfort vanished and Cassie giggled, sounding like one of Maggie's teenagers. "I just got back from visiting him. Remember when I said I was going to see my cousin? I went to Iowa. I didn't want to tell anyone the truth because of the way gossip travels in this town."

Maggie could understand that. Everyone who had come into the store the previous day had seemed to know about her hitting the jackpot. But Cassie's words disturbed her.

"You've only met him once and you're going to marry him?"

"I know him very well," Cassie shot back, her face sprouting pink spots on her round cheeks. "We talk every night on the computer."

"The computer?" Maggie's thoughts went to Billie and her online experience.

"That's how I met him." Her plump face grew more pink. "We talked for two months before he sent me a ticket to go out there. We hit it off like we had always known each other."

"You and Billie." Maggie shook her head and rolled her eyes.

Cassie giggled again. "I know she talks to guys, too. I think she's trying to find a guy, even if she won't admit it."

"I don't understand you people," Maggie said with a quick shake of her head that sent a curl tumbling across her face. She shoved it back out of her way, tucking it behind one ear.

When had the world gone so out of kilter? She'd left for Las Vegas and appeared to have entered some parallel universe. Winning that jackpot. Having these crazy sensations about Jack. Billie and her computer. And now Cassie getting married.

Cassie was grinning, a cagey, cat-who-caught-the-canary look. "You should try it."

Maggie drew back in surprise. "I don't need a man." But her thoughts flew to Jack, swirling around with outlandish fantasies. What would it be like to press against that hard chest again? To gaze up into those eyes the color of a summer sky or to have them focused on her? A man like that, not Jack, she corrected herself.

"What?" Cassie's voice was sharp as a cracking whip. "How can you say that? You're not getting any younger, Maggie."

Her fancies collapsed like a deflating balloon, complete with raspberry sound effects. "Thanks, Cassie. I don't need you to tell me that."

"Come on, be honest. You don't want to spend the rest of your life living in this rundown little house, do you?"

"I don't have to pay much rent since my parents own it, and I know all my neighbors. I like it here." That was only half true. Maggie let her gaze slide around the cramped kitchen with its yellowing linoleum floor. The house was a two bedroom bungalow, built as Air Force family housing in the late 1940s. Furnished with shabby castoffs from her parent's home, the house was all Maggie could afford, but she kept telling herself she was fine with it. Certainly at times, she thought about a house with bedrooms for both girls and a huge backyard for their sheepdog, Kayla, but for now it was just a dream. *And then Jack wouldn't be next door* a nagging little voice reminded her.

Cassie shook her head in an exaggerated motion and rolled her eyes. "Okay, but is this where you want to be the rest of your life? The only sign of the outside world is that magnet collection on your refrigerator."

Maggie's eyes rested beyond Cassie on the front of her refrigerator. Most of it was covered with magnets from all over the country. People from town brought them back from wherever they visited because they knew she collected them.

"There's not much I can do about it," Maggie said, getting to her feet, hoping that gave her babysitter the hint that she needed to get ready for work. Cassie's comments irritated her, and she was growing tired of the conversation.

Cassie hefted herself up, folding the check she'd been using as a fan and tucking it in her breast pocket. "I'm leaving next week, but say, you wouldn't need a TV or stereo, would you? I'm selling a few things I don't have room to take."

"You might check with Billie about the stereo. She was thinking of getting a new one."

"How about a computer? I'm selling that too."

That caught Maggie's interest. "You're selling your computer? How much do you want for it?"

"Only five hundred dollars, and I paid three times that. It's practically new, but I don't have room in my car, and I won't need it in Iowa."

"I might want that." A lower price for a computer left more money for other things.

"Really?" Her pudgy face lit up in a smile. "Going to look for the man of your dreams?"

"No," Maggie denied forcefully. "The girls mentioned it might be good for homework."

"Sure," Cassie replied with a coy look.

A quick rap at the kitchen door interrupted them and provided a welcome relief. Maggie could have hugged whoever was there. As it was, she found Jack standing on the back porch stoop. His presence evoked a strange tickling in her stomach that surprised her as much as the elevated pulse when she'd watched him running.

"Hi, I thought I'd check in with you about the car before you headed off for work. I can go by and get the parts this afternoon on my way home if you still want me to do that."

His smile was wide, engaging, with a dimple denting his cheek. She had not noticed it until the day before, and now she feared she would always be aware of it. Maggie's face grew warm as she gave him a nod that ended up being more vigorous than intended.

"Of course. I really need that done. Would you like to come in? Cassie and I are just chatting."

"Actually I was going to volunteer to take you to work," he offered. "That way I could drive your car and see how bad the brakes are and get a feel for what I need to fix them."

Maggie hadn't expected such thorough or quick service. "I'll finish with Cassie and meet you outside in ten minutes."

Jack skipped down the cement steps, his body tall and straight. He certainly had showered and dressed quickly. His black hair was neatly combed, though it still looked damp.

In his clothes, he presented every bit an appealing package as he had in his running shorts and form-fitting t-shirt. Broad shoulders beneath a snowy white shirt, long legs encased in regulation navy pants. He always appeared so neat, though she knew his job as a communications officer at the base required that. How could such a hunk of a man have been living next door to her for the past four years and until the day at the casino, she had never realized how physically appealing he was?

~ * ~

Jack told himself he was being foolish, this insisting he drive Maggie's car to work to check the brakes. He knew very well what parts she probably needed, and he could take the rest back if he got the wrong equipment.

But he did want to see her. Or maybe he wanted to see his own reaction to her now that they were back on familiar ground. Maggie had been his neighbor since he came to Cactus Bluffs. It was common to see her in her bathrobe coming outside for the paper, cutting the grass in torn t-shirt and shorts, chasing the dog in baggy sweatpants. He'd never had any sort of reaction to her other than the friendly exchanges they often had.

At times, he'd helped her look after the girls when her normal babysitter or Billie weren't available. Once he had cut down a dead tree and the previous spring he helped put in a patio and barbecue. She could have been any other chum or buddy he'd ever helped. But somehow today he wasn't thinking in that direction.

Maggie came out of the house, shaking her head as she walked toward him. He waited in the driveway, leaning against her Honda, which looked like it might need tires, too.

She was dressed in her normal uniform of jeans with a red-and-white striped shirt. But today he found himself noting the gentle swell of her breasts, the rounded curves of her hips in the tight jeans. Jack forced his gaze up to her face as an unwelcome shiver ran down his back.

Her expression was disturbed, her brow furrowed, and curls the color of pale ale danced around her head. She blinked as her eyes rose to meet his as though she'd been deep in thought and was surprised to see him.

"Something wrong?" he asked as she unlocked the car doors.

"Not really. Cassie's getting married and leaving town. Now I'm going to have to find another babysitter for the girls."

"They're thirteen now. Aren't they able to take care of themselves?" he asked.

"Well, it's okay during the day and the early evening, but once a month I have to work a week of night shifts, and I hate the thought of leaving them on their own until midnight or one in the morning." She tossed her purse into the back seat of the car and climbed into the driver's side.

He slid onto the front passenger seat, folding his long legs so that his knees bumped up against the front dashboard. He was going to have a hell of a time driving this thing. He pushed the seat back so that he had more leg room.

"She's marrying someone she met on the internet," Maggie continued, shaking her head more vehemently. She appeared rather agitated, her face flushed.

"Okay," he said, not certain what was really on her mind or what reaction she expected.

"Can you believe that?" Maggie's voice was filled with disbelief and as she turned toward him, her brown eyes were filled with surprise behind the thick glasses. "She talked to him on the computer, met him once and now she's going to marry him."

Her shocked outrage was innocent and in a way, appealing. He couldn't help but smile. "I've heard it happens a lot. I thought Billie was trying to convince you to get online and meet men yesterday."

The question was meant to be teasing, but Jack found himself curious about her response. Again Maggie blinked, eyes sweeping down as the pink flush deepened. Had he ever before noticed how perfect her cheeks were? Right now they were the color of a dish of strawberry ice cream.

Her lips twitched with irritation, but that look didn't bother him. Actually he found it endearing. *Whoa.* He needed to slow down here. Finding her traits attractive was taking a step beyond being a friend.

Her head was shaking, amber curls hopping up and down on her head like twirling corkscrews.

"I couldn't do that." She faced him suddenly with those wide eyes, looking very curious. "Have you ever flirted online?"

Jack drew back, her question catching him off guard. "Well..."

"You have a computer, right? Online access? Isn't that why the girls go over and borrow your computer?"

"Yes," he admitted, embarrassment making his cheeks burn. "But I don't use my computer as a social tool." He had heard the stories of lonely men spending their nights online, looking for romance. Some men at the base admitted doing that. He preferred meeting women in person. When he had women in his life. Or more correctly, should he ever have a woman in his life. He couldn't imagine it happening any time soon.

"I don't think I could either," she said.

"Well, I think it's a good idea for you to have one. Not that I wouldn't miss your girls' visits. They make life interesting when they're around."

Her face lit up proudly, a smile drawing up her full pink lips. "Yes, they do."

The smile sent a buzz of electricity through him and he turned to look out the window. Luckily they were turning the corner that would lead them to the convenience store. "Did you tell them about the possibility of buying a computer?"

"It's what they want." Her voice sounded uncertain.

"I gather you don't think it's a good idea?" he asked, glancing back at her.

Her face clouded over and her lips pressed into a scowl. "They want to use it to look for their father. I don't know if that's good."

At times he feared they might be doing something like that on his computer, but he never left them alone for long. Not having parental controls on his machine, Jack made a point of keeping a steady watch on them.

"You don't think that's a good idea?" he asked.

"Not searching for him. If Al is coming back, he'll do it on his own." She said it with such a pronounced emphasis, he wasn't about to argue.

"I understand. But I know that people have found long lost friends and relatives online. One of my old high school buddies looked me up a couple of months ago."

"He found you on the internet?" she asked, her face whipping toward him.

"Well, yes."

"So Al could find us," she said. Her eyes grew wide and danced with excitement. "If he's been wondering where I am, he could find me on the computer."

Three

The convenience store was empty while a lone car sat at the pumps. The driver had already brought in his ten dollars. Maggie worked at refilling jars of beef jerky before turning her attention to straightening the boxes of candy on the counter. No matter how careful she and Billie tried to be, customers constantly picked up things and put them down somewhere else or rifled through the candy boxes.

"I'm thinking of buying Cassie's computer," Maggie called across the store.

"Great idea. I didn't know she was selling one." Billie was working in the snack bar area, wiping down white laminated tables and the plastic chairs around them.

"She came by this morning and told me she met some guy on the computer and is going to marry him."

"See? I told you it happens," Billie replied. She stopped her work and pushed red hair from her face. "If Cassie can find a guy online, anyone can."

Maggie shook her head, frowning across at Billie. "I don't think that computer stuff is for me, but I might go ahead and get it for the girls."

Almost as though on cue, April and May burst through the glass doors, trailed by Cassie. Maggie was not surprised by the girls' visit. They often stopped on their way home from school, but Cassie's presence was unusual. She took care of the girls in the evening and at night.

"Hi, Mom," April sang out. "We thought we'd come by and get something to munch on."

Maggie held up a granola bar and waved it at them. "No chocolate," she admonished, but as always, she felt proud at the sight of her two girls.

April and May were fraternal twins, born within hours of each other. April had been born in the waning hours of April while May had been born right after midnight. They were as different as the months.

April was not only older, but the more outspoken and daring of the pair. She had her father's blue-green eyes, silky blonde hair and wide, toothy smile. May was quiet with an innate wisdom that she used to calm down her older sister. She had Maggie's brown eyes and Maggie's sandy-colored hair. Both were tall and leggy, taking after their father. Already they'd shot up past Maggie's five-foot-three-inch height. Luckily, it looked as though they would inherit Maggie's flawless skin.

Ever the obedient one, May picked up a granola bar, but April approached the candy display of gummy bears.

"No sugar without nutritional value," Maggie added.

As the girls dug through the displays, Cassie walked up to the counter. "I was talking to the girls about the computer..."

"May we get it, Mom?" April asked. "Please, pleeeese?"

Maggie normally found it hard to say no to her daughter when she stretched out the word 'please' like that. Across the store, Billie watched the exchange without saying anything. Maggie knew her opinion and was thankful her friend didn't add to the pressure. She would have preferred that Cassie not mention the computer offer until Maggie made up her mind.

She drew a deep breath, forcing her annoyance inward. "We can talk about it over dinner."

"It can be handy for lots of things," Cassie offered. It was obvious she was in a rush to get it sold.

"We could use it to do our homework," May pointed out, the ever-practical one. "And if we get some games, it might keep us from going to the arcade as much."

Maggie doubted that. Their trips to the arcade were usually to meet friends. Still, she looked from one to the other and then at Billie, who was again cleaning the snack tables as though she wasn't the least bit interested in the conversation.

"Cassie has it in her car," April added. "She can take it over and help us set it up right now."

That explained Cassie's sudden presence at the store. The plump babysitter had obviously decided she could make the sale if she could line up the girls as allies. Maggie had to admit it was a good deal, but she didn't like the pressure Cassie was bringing to bear.

"Let me think about it," she said.

April approached the counter and put a bag of trail mix and two granola bars on the counter. "See? I'm being good," she offered.

Maggie smiled at her daughter. April, the ever-lively twin, would probably behave just long enough to get her to agree. Both girls retreated to the back of the store to get soda.

"You won't be sorry," Cassie spoke up. "It's a lucky computer. Maybe you'll meet someone wonderful on it like I did."

Maggie's irritation with Cassie was at the boiling point. "I don't think so. I have no interest in finding a man. I told you that. I'm fine with my girls. If I get that computer, it's for them, not so I can go online and make a fool of myself looking for love." She immediately regretted her waspish words and looked to the back of the store where the girls were arguing over soda flavors, pleased they hadn't heard her comment.

At the same time, a jingling rang out. The door was opening and a customer was walking inside.

She was aware of Cassie staring at her with a hurt expression, making her feel worse. She opened her mouth to apologize, but Cassie spoke up first.

"You know your problem, Maggie? You just don't want to admit that Al Williams is never coming back."

It was like being slapped across the face. Maggie drew back, shocked and surprised. She turned away from Cassie. Even though people might know about him, no one ever mentioned the name. Maggie might still have her dreams of him coming to take her out of Cactus Bluffs, just as she had them when she had been seventeen years old, but no one had ever mentioned it out loud to her face.

As she turned away from Cassie, she saw the customer who had entered. Jack looked from one to the other, a look of shock on his handsome face.

Billie marched forward from the snack area, taking control of the situation. "Cassie, that's a horrible thing to say."

"I'm sorry," Cassie said quickly, voice filled with regret. "I didn't mean that."

"It's okay," Maggie said, pushing her glasses up her nose. She could feel her cheeks turning warm, but she tried to act as though it didn't matter, though she couldn't meet Billie's, Cassie's or Jack's eyes. She rolled her shoulders in a shrug. "I know he isn't coming back."

Jack walked forward as if he hadn't heard the exchange, though she knew he had. He offered a wide smile, cutting through the tense air.

"Well, well, afternoon ladies." He looked as crisp and fresh as he had nearly eight hours earlier when he had dropped her off at work. His black hair gleamed under the harsh store lights and unlike the splotches on her vest and shirt, his white shirt was still spotless and unwrinkled. His quick, warm smile sent a strange buzz through her.

Then something else hit Maggie—a rather unwelcome distraction. "Hey, Kayla!"

"What?" Billie said.

"It just occurred to me. I haven't seen Kayla since I got back yesterday. Usually she wakes up when I come home at night, but last night she didn't come out of her dog house. I didn't see her this morning, either, when I filled up her water dish."

Kayla was a black and white sheepdog that Al had given Maggie before he'd left. Maggie always thought it meant Al would be back. A man wouldn't just leave his dog. It was a sign of commitment to her. But she hadn't seen the dog since she'd left for Las Vegas, and a pang of panic rushed through her.

She turned to Jack. "Did you see her this morning?" During the day, the big dog spent as much time lounging under Jack's big elm shade tree as she did in Maggie's yard. She'd forged her own hole in the slats of the fence to go back and forth at will.

He blinked rapidly, lifting his head as though considering the thought, then shook his head. "Not this morning. I thought she might be inside the house since she didn't go running with me."

Maggie's head jerked toward the girls who were coming forward, each with a big bottle of iced tea and another of diet soda. They put their choices on the front counter and turned to Jack as Maggie began to ring up their purchases. Dick would let the girls take anything they wanted for free as long as Maggie rang them up, but she always made a point of paying him back when she got her paycheck.

"Did you girls remember to feed Kayla last night? Have either one of you seen her today?" she asked. "Jack hasn't seen her and neither have I."

They exchanged suddenly concerned glances. Feeding and watering Kayla was one of their chores, though Maggie often had to remind them. Surely they wouldn't forget such a big responsibility when Maggie was out of town, would they? Kayla had her tags, and everyone in town knew her, but what if she had wandered off? What if she had ventured near the highway?

"I haven't seen her since yesterday morning before school," April admitted.

"We need to look for her," May added. She cast a beseeching glance at Jack. "Will you help us?"

"Sure, let's go," Jack said. He patted Maggie on the shoulder, a touch that surprised her with its gentleness as well as shocked her because of the way it quickened her pulse. "Don't worry, Maggie. We'll find her. I can come back and get you later."

"What about the computer?" Cassie asked in a whiny voice, as the other three disappeared out the door.

Maggie was pleased that the dog search had grabbed the girls' attention. Now she could make the decision without her daughters' pressure. At the same time, she was still perturbed with Cassie for the Al Williams remark. And shouldn't the babysitter have made certain the girls fed the dog and knew where it was? No, she was being unfair. Kayla was the twins' responsibility.

"I don't know," Maggie said with a sigh. She glanced at Billie, who was shaking her head.

"You know what I think."

"It is a bargain," she admitted, nodding at Cassie. "Okay, we'll take it."

~ * ~

"Are you all right?" Jack asked as he and Maggie walked along the street, flicking their flashlights from one direction to the next.

They had spent the early evening searching the streets around the house, calling for Kayla. Now darkness had fallen, and the dog remained missing. They extended the search to the edges of the highways that intersected in the middle of town. No one would say it, but Jack knew they all feared the same thing. The old, slow dog might have been trying to cross and been hit by one of the speeding motorists that zoomed through town.

"I'm fine," Maggie said, but irritation lurked in her voice.

She had not said much through their rushed dinner of tuna sandwiches. Jack had helped the girls prepare the dinner so they could all resume the hunt. The girls had gone toward the west side of town along one highway while he and Maggie searched the north-south section of the other main road.

"We'll find her," he said. "Or she'll come home."

"I hope." Her voice remained tense. She shifted her flashlight from side to side, her head down.

"You really love that dog," he said with a chuckle, trying to lighten the mood. "How old is she?"

"Fourteen, maybe almost fifteen. I don't know."

"So you've had her since high school?"

"Right after. Uh... Al gave her to me."

Jack wanted to kick himself. How stupid was that? He should have guessed it. All those years he had lived next to her and he had never known that. Well, now that the subject was in the open…

"Cassie was kind of rough on you today. Making that comment about Al."

Her lip twitched in irritation, but she didn't respond. Maybe he shouldn't have said anything, but he had felt bad for her at the time. Her face had been very pink, and for an instant he'd thought he had seen tears cloud her chocolate eyes behind her large glasses.

"I'm sorry. I guess it's none of my business," he added. Jack wanted to touch her arm, but held back. They'd never been close before, and he wasn't quite sure she would welcome it now. She had seemed to tense earlier when he'd patted her shoulder.

"Do you suppose everyone in town feels that way?" she asked, voice filled with resigned sadness.

"What way?"

"Poor old Maggie, waiting for Al Williams to come back? I suppose if he was coming, he would have done so already."

Jack drew a sharp breath. He hated to hurt her, but he had been thinking the same thing. "I don't know. I've never been much for gossip."

She gave him a grateful smile, and he found his blood growing warm. "Thanks for that, but everyone knows the story. Al was an Air Force mechanic. He was stationed here for two years, but I only got to know him the last six months he was here. He's never come back. He left me with Kayla and the girls."

"So he never knew about the twins?"

Her lip twitched again. "He knew. I told him the night before he left. Well, he didn't know they were twins. I didn't even know then. I hoped he might stay. Either get a delay in his transfer or send for me. He promised he would give me his new address once he got to Florida…" She stopped and he realized tears were pouring down her cheeks.

"I'm sorry," he said. Without thinking he reached down and gently wiped her damp cheek with his fingers. The skin was as soft as a fresh, ripe peach. A spark of excitement coursed though his blood, elevating his body temperature to unwanted heights. He put his other arm on her shoulder, feeling uncertain and yet wanting to console her.

She pulled slightly away, pulling off her glasses and wiping her eyes. "You must think I'm such a fool. After all these years…"

He dropped his hand, but kept his arm on her shoulder, rubbing it gently. "No. I understand you. What I don't understand is why he didn't come back."

"You don't think I'm an idiot?" Her head stayed down, eyes refusing to meet his. "I thought he would come back. Year after year, I waited. It used to be that every time the bell rang at the store, I'd jump, or if a man with blonde hair came to the pumps I'd be checking him out on the surveillance camera. Oh, hell, sometimes I still do."

She shook her head and her curls hopped. He touched one, soft and silky as cornsilk.

"I do understand," he repeated softly, thinking of his own predicament. He dropped his hand from her, suddenly feeling disloyal for even touching her. "I used to look for Carla in crowds. And I knew she was gone. I watched her die, but some part of me wanted to believe she wasn't dead, and that she might come back to me."

She looked up at him in wonder. Soft fingers brushed his cheek as he had touched hers. The fleeting touch sent a wave of electricity through his blood. "I'm sorry," she said in a hushed tone.

He wanted to catch her hand, hold it, but the specter of Carla hung over him, as though she might be watching his admission. "I've come to accept that she's gone. But it's why I came here, to Cactus Bluffs. I wanted to be some place that was as different from Washington as possible. That was where we shared our life together, so I wanted to be in a place where I couldn't imagine her. She hated the hot, dry weather. It's almost like she would be with me if I was back in Washington. Does that make sense?" He couldn't believe he was revealing these personal thoughts, and yet he had seen Maggie soothe her girls and so many others over the years. He trusted her with his heartfelt admission.

She dropped her hand and turned away. "Yes, it does. Like I said, I did wait for Al. Sometimes I think that's why I don't leave this place, because I know if he wants to find me, he'll know where to look."

He inhaled sharply. He wanted to catch her hand, hold it. In a way they were both alike, trapped in the past.

A horn blared as a car came around a bend. April's head leaned out the door.

"Mom, we found her! We found Kayla."

Their moments of closeness vanished in the pressure of the present. They hurried to the red Firebird that he recognized as belonging to Billie.

"Where?" Maggie asked as April emerged from the front seat and Jack replaced her. The two climbed in the back with May.

"It's my fault," April said apologetically. "I must have locked her in the storage shed by mistake when I put away my bike. We found her tonight when I opened it to get out our bikes to look for her."

Maggie sighed heavily. "You should be more careful. You're growing up. You need to take more responsibility. Especially now."

"Yes, Mom," April agreed. "Why now?"

"Well, with Cassie leaving, you may be on your own more. I don't know how I'm going to afford another babysitter."

"I can look after them," Jack found himself offering. "You said you only need help that week when you're working the late shift. I can watch television over there as easily as I can do it at home."

"And if you get them that computer, I can guarantee they'll be staying home more," Billie commented.

"Did you decide to get it?" April asked, her voice rising a notch.

Maggie sighed deeply. "Yes, but I don't want you on it all the time."

Their shrieks rang out in the car, even as she touched his shoulder. "Thank you, Jack. I'll pay you, of course."

"It's fine," he said. "We can talk about that later." The girls were still chattering and he wondered if he wasn't getting himself in over his head. Being the kindly neighbor was one thing, but playing babysitter to a couple of rambunctious teenage girls was something else.

Wait until the guys at the base heard about this. They'd think he was losing his mind. But they had their families. There were times loneliness overtook him at night and he had nothing but the television, his books or computer for company. At times, Jack listened for the noise of their loud music next door, or their giggles out in the yard when they played. In some ways, Maggie and her girls had become the closest thing he'd ever had to a family.

He looked up and found she was staring at his reflection in the rearview mirror. He offered her a smile and when she smiled back, he again felt that crazy sensation that tightened his stomach and buzzed in his head.

~ * ~

Maggie watched Cassie drive away in her old Honda from behind a lacy curtain. Behind her, the computer sat on the kitchen table, the monitor, keyboard, scanner and printer all resting beside it. Cassie called it her lucky computer. The thought of the overweight woman with the acne-ravaged face and big nose going off to marry the man of her dreams still rankled slightly, though Maggie wasn't certain why. Maybe it was because Cassie raised the prospect that dreams could come true.

Until the night before, Maggie had never admitted to anyone--even Billie--about her dreams of Al returning to Cactus Bluffs, though she suspected her friend knew that was what she wanted. What had Jack thought when she said those crazy things?

She touched a finger to her cheek, recalling his gentle touch and the churning in her stomach at the feel of it. Suddenly she had been aware of the strong, tanned forearms at eye level and the clean, musky scent of his cologne.

Today, embarrassment replaced that jumpy feeling as she recalled what she admitted to him about Al. Maggie had always presented herself to the people of the town as not caring about her lack of a love life. But at times, she lay awake at night thinking of how badly she wanted Al to come rescue her and the girls from their life in the doldrums. Her talk with Jack had her thinking. Should she give up that dream and look elsewhere? Was she wrong in waiting for Al?

Maggie looked down at herself. Was she that bad? She had a little extra padding on her hips and thighs and a spare tire growing around her middle, but that wasn't anything that couldn't be fixed with a little dieting.

Her glasses were thick, but she could wear contacts if she wanted. That was just another added expense she couldn't afford at the moment. Her hair was what she considered a dull shade of blonde but with its natural curl and body, she thought it could look good when she took time to style it. The color stood out when she put highlights into it, but she'd never been able to afford to keep it colored professionally. Her skin was her best feature. It had always been smooth and flawless, which was lucky for her. Make-up was so expensive, Maggie seldom wore any.

Billie was always saying she could be decent looking if she worked on her appearance, but Maggie never tried. Why bother? The man of her dreams was familiar with her looks.

Turning around, Maggie picked up the computer and its components and carried them into what had once been the formal dining room. It had long ago been combined with the living room to make a larger family room. She was going to set up the computer at a table in a corner because both girls would want to use it. Their room was too small for a desk; they'd always done their homework on two varnished planks her father had set up on top of file cabinets in the old dining room. The computer would go at the end of the makeshift desks.

As Maggie completed her task, her mind flew back to the day she had sat with Billie at her computer. The one thing that had hit Maggie right away had been Billie's total lack of honesty.

"These guys don't want to hear about me as I am," Billie had explained. "No one wants to hear about this place. I give them a dream. I can be anything I want on here."

Maggie stared at the various parts of the computer as she finished. Could it be the magic wizard everyone seemed to think it was? No. She couldn't be dishonest like Billie. And she doubted she would find someone special, like Cassie.

She brushed aside those thoughts as more practical questions hit her. Who was going to hook up this thing? She had no idea how to make complicated things work. Her father had connected the TV and DVD player, but he wouldn't know what to do with a computer. Billie had flirted with an engineer from the base to get hers to work. Well, maybe Jack could come over and help them set up the computer.

Jack! Thoughts of him had been coming and going all day. Mainly she thought of his touches, the gentleness of those fingers that she couldn't have imagined. But there was more to her thoughts of him than physical sensations. She appreciated his offer to babysit. At least she wouldn't need his help today. She'd worked the early shift and would be home when the girls arrived in an hour.

Shaking her hands as though that might erase her thoughts, she grimaced. *Darn it!* She had to stop this foolishness. She needed to forget about Jack and her crazy thoughts. His touches were meant as nothing more than soothing her. He still loved his wife. She could hear it in his voice as he talked about her.

Maggie had wanted to tell him he needed to start living again, to try to find a new love, but the words had died on her lips. Who was she to try to impose such rules on others? What about herself? Shouldn't she hold those same rules for her own life?

Her eyes fell on the green screen of the computer monitor. Could the answer be somewhere in there? Despite her doubts, could she use the computer, as Cassie had, to meet someone special?

Four

"Thanks for the help," Maggie said to Jack, as he stood from the folding chair in front of the computer. His tall figure hovered next to her, and an odd excitement sparked inside her, making her conscious of his hard chest covered by a tight t-shirt as he remained near her. His well-muscled arms, tanned from days doing yard work, hovered near eye level. Feeling hypnotized, she pulled her eyes away from him, though his masculine scent lingered in her nostrils.

"It's up and running," he announced, waving at the chair. "Who's first?"

"Me!" April exclaimed, sliding into the chair one step ahead of May, who tossed her an angry look.

"You know you're just going to play games," she admonished.

"So?" April challenged, positioning the keyboard in front of her and then clicking on the mouse. "Like you were going to do homework?"

April's fingers flew over the keyboard and worked the mouse until the screen filled with images.

Maggie watched with interest and then turned to Jack in surprise. "She looks like she knows what she's doing."

His wide grin and sudden wink sent shivers of awareness through her. "She does. She's been playing games at my house."

Maggie's cheeks grew warm, which meant she was probably blushing. Sometimes she hated her fair skin because it colored so easily and noticeably. She brushed her hand across her cheek, as though that would erase any pink that might stain her cheek. "Well, you've come through for us again," she said, unable to meet his eyes. "I don't know how to thank you."

"I hope you all enjoy it."

Her gaze traveled back to the machine. "I doubt I'll use it much. I'm really not very good when it comes to dealing with mechanical things." Thoughts of Billie and her proficiency in using her computer buzzed through her head. Maggie knew she would never be that good.

"I don't believe that. I've watched you work that register."

His praise ignited warm sensations inside her, even as the touch scorched her. Was he flirting with her? No, not Jack. He was merely being nice.

"I better be going," he said, shifting from one foot to the next.

"You should stay for dinner," Maggie suggested. "I got home early and cooked up a big pan of lasagna." She stopped, embarrassment overcoming her. It was as though she was pleading with him to stay.

"And I'm going to make a salad." May's blonde head popped up from leaning over her sister's shoulder at the computer. "We have to have something healthy in this house. Too much lasagna and I'll gain weight."

~ * ~

After dinner the girls concentrated on homework at the kitchen table, while Jack offered to show Maggie how to operate the computer and get online. She sat in front of the computer, trying not to look too baffled. Jack's large masculine frame hovered over her, elevating her pulse. She kept her face averted from him, fearing he could see the effect he had on her.

She'd found herself studying him through dinner, noticing more things than she should have. His wide forehead, the chiseled cheeks which were slightly darkened by stubble, the firm, square jaw were all familiar to her, but she'd never realized what a nice overall package they presented. He was handsome, and not just boy-next-door handsome, but outright good looking. How had she missed that all these years?

"The computer is great for research," he was saying, long fingers clicking on the mouse. His fingers brushed hers, sending a raw burst of energy racing through her. Maggie pulled her hands to her lap and folded them, hoping he didn't see her sudden case of trembling.

"And you can look for men, like Cassie," April called from the kitchen.

Maggie shook her head, hair flying around her face. Beside her, Jack's body grew stiff. "I'd never do that," she said.

"We could look for our dad," April called.

The twins had mentioned it when they were discussing buying a computer, but hadn't mentioned it since. Maggie was surprised it had come up again. "I don't know about that."

April's face appeared at the door. "Jill at school said her mom was adopted, and she used the computer to look for her real parents. Maybe we could find our dad."

The two girls knew little about their father, except that he had left, and Maggie expected him to come back someday. Only to them had she admitted her dream.

"What do you think?" May asked, appearing beside April in the door, her young face filled with questions and hope. "Could we do some checking?"

"I don't know," Maggie said, but her heart had begun thumping faster and for once, it had nothing to do with Jack's presence beside her. Was that possible? Could they find Al? She recalled what Jack had told her about his high school friend finding him.

"I suppose maybe we could put our names out there, so he could find us if he wanted," she said.

April nodded, her young face filled with eagerness. "That's a great idea."

Maggie twisted in her chair to glance at Jack who was still playing with the mouse, pulling up things on the computer. He acted as though he had not followed the conversation.

"This is what's known as a search engine," he told her. "You can go here and put in any subject or name, and it will bring up the information."

She was almost tempted to ask him to put in Al's name, but it didn't make sense that it would come up.

"But how would you put in my name?" she asked, pushing back from the desk to give him room to show her what she wanted. "You know, so if someone was looking for me they could find me?"

Maggie thought she detected a trace of irritation in the quick twitching of his lips, but Jack clicked on a couple of icons and pulled up a blank form. He leaned forward and typed in her name. "How much information do you want to put in here?"

"Just the basics."

"It wants to know interests, age, appearance, things like that."

"Make up something great," April said, leaning on the door jam. "Like young, single woman, looking to meet the man of her dreams."

"April!" Maggie threw her daughter a warning look.

"Well, that's how Cassie did it. Do you think she admitted she was overweight, living in a desert town with her folks? She said she was single, living in Southern California and loved to travel. Then, when men talked to her online, she always claimed she was fifty pounds lighter than she really was."

Maggie shook her head. "I wouldn't do that." She could almost hear Billie in her head chastising her and a little voice of her own nagged at her in the back of her head. If she put in the truth, would Al want to come back?

~ * ~

Hours later Maggie sat alone in front of the computer, thoughts going in a different direction. Maybe she could find Al. Looking around the darkened living room as though someone might be watching, she leaned close to the keyboard and typed his name into the search engine, just as Jack had showed her. An hourglass flashed on the monitor, then the screen filled with names and addresses.

Dejection touched Maggie as she stared at the response. Five hundred and ten names fit her search request. The name Al Williams was much more common than she'd anticipated. The first name was in New Jersey. Could he be there? The next was in Florida. She clicked on that name and it took her to a web page. Pictures of a balding man and his antique car came up on the screen. This was not her Al. She went to several other web pages, all with the same result. Did she want to go to five hundred more websites? Some didn't have pictures. She sighed deeply. This was going nowhere.

Maybe Cassie and Billie were right. Maybe she should try to meet someone new. All these years, she had waited for Al, and it had gotten her nowhere, but maybe she was wrong. And what could this hurt anyway?

Billie's idea of visiting chat rooms provided a starting point. Like before, it confused her more than anything. Not able to think of anything to say, Maggie simply watched the lines of conversation flash by. As she debated whether she should get out of the chat room and start searching again, a small screen appeared at the corner of her monitor. Someone was talking to her.

> *Bobcat: Hi there!*

Carefully she typed back.

> *MaggieMay: Hello, how are you?*
> *Bobcat: I'm fine, but I have a question for you. Are*
> *you my dream girl?*

Maggie wrinkled her nose at the screen. She wasn't so certain about flirting with men online. What could she say?

> *MaggieMay: I don't know.*
> *Bobcat: You seem like a real person.*
> *MaggieMay: Pretty darn real.*
> *Bobcat: Good. I am not into plastic people.*
> *MaggieMay: Pinching myself. Ouch! No, I am not*
> *plastic!*
> *Bobcat: Good.*

Maggie stared hard at the screen. She couldn't believe she had written that. Well, why not? Like Billie had said, no one knew what she looked like. She glanced at the chat room screen. She did not see Bobcat's name.

> *MaggieMay: How did you find me?*
> *Bobcat: I was looking in the directory. I hope you don't mind.*
> *MaggieMay: Not at all. I'm new to this.*
> *Bobcat: Do you want to talk?*
> *MaggieMay: I guess so. Just take it slow. I am not a good typist.*
> *Bobcat: For my dream girl, I will do anything!*

~ * ~

The morning sun inched over the far eastern horizon, a blazing ball that streaked its rays through the Venetian blinds. Maggie squirmed in the hard folding chair in front of the computer, her eyes red-rimmed and reduced to a squint. She had remained online all night, exploring a fascinating new world.

Chastising herself that she should get off, Maggie was about to click on the sign-off button when a new person sent a message saying hello. What was a few more minutes? Stifling a yawn, Maggie eagerly typed back.

> *MaggieMay: Morning.*
> *JoeP: You're up early.*
> *MaggieMay: Yes! How are you?*
> *JoeP: Fine. Do you have a picture?*
> *MaggieMay: Not to send.*
> *JoeP: Measurements?*

Maggie didn't like it when they asked for that immediately. One thing she had learned in the past twelve hours--men who started with questions about appearance had one thing on their minds.

She typed in that she would rather not give them and waited for his response. Sometimes it didn't matter and the conversation continued.

This time there was no answer. She typed in another question, but still got no response from JoeP. He was no longer interested. Several men had done the same thing after she described herself. She hated to sign off on such a sour note, but suddenly another message screen opened up.

> *Ricardo: How are you this morning?*
> *MaggieMay: I am doing great, thanks. How about you??*
> *Ricardo: Just waking up. Why aren't you here to fix my coffee?*
> *MaggieMay: Why aren't you here to fix mine?*
> *Ricardo: Ah! Feisty. I like feisty, or is it just that you haven't had your coffee yet?*
> *MaggieMay: It's both. I snarl until I get caffeine.*
> *Ricardo: Uh oh. I'm in trouble. Get her a cup of coffee quick!*

"Mom, are you on there already?"

Maggie jumped at the sound of April's voice from the hallway door. She twisted around to look at her daughter, who lounged against the door jam, blonde hair falling around her face in stringy clumps and eyes heavy with sleep.

Reaching over to switch off the lamp beside her, Maggie fought off a yawn and gave her daughter as bright a smile as she could muster. No sense letting April know she was not just getting online--she'd been on since the twins had gone to bed.

"Morning, sweetie," she said as April disappeared down the hall and through the bathroom door. She had not intended to be online all night. Somehow it had just happened. It was as though the door to a strange new world had opened up to her as Maggie had visited chat room after chat room. As she'd grown more comfortable, she'd even talked in a few.

She'd had several personal conversations as well. In addition to Bobcat, who was in construction, Maggie had talked to a midnight watchman in North Carolina and a bookkeeper from Maine. There had been a clerk from Northern California, a rancher from Texas, a policeman from Oklahoma and a woman who worked in a convenience store in Kentucky. None of the conversations had lasted long, and when some of the men had made improper requests, Maggie stopped talking to them. At first, that had been frightening, and then she'd realized none of the men knew where she was, so they couldn't find her.

April came out of the hall and crossed to the kitchen.

"You'd better get your sister up," Maggie said.

Usually it was the other way around. April would sleep in and May would have to get her going in the morning.

"May got me up," April announced. "She's getting dressed. I told her I'd get her some juice. Mom, why did you close the door to the hall?"

The door usually remained open, but Maggie had closed it so they would not know she was still up or what she was doing once it got past midnight.

A tap on the back door stopped her from having to answer. It also pulled her away from the computer. She knew it would be Jack, and she quickly hit the sign-off key. No sense letting him think she'd been online all night.

"You'd better get ready for school," she admonished as her daughter walked back across the room. April glumly nodded and headed back down the hall, carrying two glasses of orange juice.

Maggie approached the door, threw it open and smiled at Jack. As usual he looked crisp and efficient, even at six in the morning. He wore creased khaki pants, white shirt and black tie. His short, black hair was neatly combed.

A bout of self consciousness swept through her. Her terrycloth robe had been white at one time, but now it was a sick shade of gray and little holes dotted the arm where Kayla had gotten hold of it one day. But it was preferable to letting him see her pajamas, which had once been pink and now were faded and fraying around the collar.

Pulling her tattered robe around her, Maggie pushed open the door. "What are you doing up so early this morning?"

His wide grin set her heart to thumping. "I saw your light on when I got up. I'm doing an early shift today and I thought I'd see if you want me to pick up the car at noon and take it over to get the parts we need."

She brushed her hair behind her ear, aware it was probably unruly and frizzy this time of morning. Could he tell she had not been to bed all night? Should it matter?

"Well, yes, that's fine," she said, attempting a smile and then abandoning it when it threatened to evolve into a yawn.

"You can keep the car all weekend if you want. Billie's taking us to Los Angeles in the morning to do some shopping. How much for the parts?" Realizing she was rambling, Maggie stopped.

He twisted halfway around, his gaze resting on the car that sat in the driveway. Its gray paint dusty and faded by the blistering desert sun, it looked like it was in need of a friend.

"I'll give you the bill later, and I'll try to keep it at a minimum," he said.

She nodded gratefully. "I trust you, Jack. And I do appreciate it. You'll have to come over for dinner again." Maybe she shouldn't have made the offer, but Maggie had been thinking about his comments that he still looked for his dead wife in crowds.

She'd never thought Jack might be lonely, but his actions at times were those of a man looking for something to do. Men from the base were always asking for his help and he readily gave it. His offers to help the girls with the yard work came so often that it sometimes made her feel guilty.

Their talk as they had looked for Kayla had given her new insight into his life and posed some questions in her mind. Why didn't he have a girlfriend or at least look for one? He was a nice looking man with a good personality and a generous nature, but he never frequented the few local bars where Air Force men hung out looking to meet women in Cactus Bluffs. Was it because he still grieved for his wife? Maggie had seen a picture of the woman in his living room, and she was beautiful.

Jack's eyes were on the car, and at first he didn't give an indication that he'd heard her invitation. Suddenly he turned toward her and nodded abruptly. "I'd like that."

"Look, Jack, I'm not sure about this charging me later for the parts. Why don't I write you a check now and you can cash it when you get the parts? That way, the money doesn't have to come out of your pocket."

Maggie moved back so he could step inside. As he moved past her, the clean scent of sandalwood soap wafted to her nostrils. She'd noticed it before, but this time, her pulse quickened. Drawing a deep breath to let the scent wash over her, Maggie led him to the desk where she normally wrote her bills, next to the computer.

He seemed to notice that it was on, and to her horror, the screen showed she was still signed on. Ricardo had been saying hello and asking Maggie if she still wanted to talk.

A sly smile crossed Jack's face and he gestured at the screen. "Admit it, you've been on there all night."

Heat flooded Maggie's cheeks, and she vigorously shook her head, but he chuckled.

He tilted his head and the corners of his eyes crinkled as they danced with mischief. "Are you sure? I went to bed at midnight and your light was on. When I got up an hour ago, your light was already on. Tell the truth," he said in a teasing tone.

She shoved her glasses up her nose. Even without the telltale lamp, he could probably tell from her bloodshot eyes that she had been online all night.

"Well, okay. Maybe I was on there for quite a while."

His quick laugh was warm and not the least bit patronizing. "Don't be embarrassed. I did the same thing when I got my new computer. I was going from website to website. Suddenly I had tons of things I wanted to look up."

Maggie didn't dare tell him she'd spent the night talking to people, not looking up things. What would he think of her?

He chucked her playfully on the chin and the touch was like being branded by a red-hot iron. Her breath caught, and she turned away, fearing he might notice her overreaction.

"I hope you were doing more than just talking to guys online," he said.

Her cheeks went from warm to red hot, and she shifted from one foot to the next.

"Why, Maggie, you're blushing." His voice was soft, almost hypnotic.

She licked her lips and let her eyes drift up to meet his. The blue eyes twinkled with glee. Why hadn't she ever noticed what an attractive man he was? All that talk with those men overnight was fun, but were any of them as nice as Jack? Any as pleasant or good looking?

His close proximity, the teasing smile and the scent of the sandalwood soap had her heart racing now. Maggie slid into the chair, fumbling for her checkbook.

"I'll turn that off," she said and this time she managed to hit the correct buttons to shut down the computer.

May stumbled down the hall, empty juice glass in hand. "Morning Mom. Can you tell April to hurry up and get out of the shower? Hi, Jack."

"Good morning, May."

Maggie glanced in Jack's direction, but could not meet his eyes. "Please don't tell the girls I was on there all night," she whispered. "Or that I was talking to anyone." Her vision on the checkbook faltered, lines floating in front of her. She reached under her glasses and rubbed her aching eyes. She was going to have a tough day at work. How would she ever stay awake? Maybe she could take a nap after the girls left.

Beside her, Jack shifted. Maggie sneaked a look, noticing that his eyes were no longer dancing and had become serious. A frown creased his handsome, chiseled face. "You weren't looking for Al, were you?"

"I did at first, but there are hundreds of Al Williams. He could be anywhere, from Connecticut to Florida to Alaska."

"Then you were looking." His voice bordered on accusing.

"I think he deserves to know about both his daughters, don't you?" she asked, irritation sparking inside her.

Jack drew back as though she had hit him. "I guess," he said tersely.

She chewed on her lower lip, feeling guilty for being so touchy. Maybe it was because she was tired. "You and I are a lot alike. You've always played it safe, haven't you?"

"There's nothing wrong with that."

"No, I guess not. But this week, I took a big gamble. I put in all my money and I won a jackpot. Maybe I should try that more often. I've felt like a loser for most of my life. Maybe my luck has finally changed. Maybe I'm on the verge of a winning streak."

Five

DreamGirl: Do you remember me? We were talking the other day. My name was MaggieMay then.

Ricardo: Maggie, my girl. I remember. You took off on me. Like you had a better offer.

DreamGirl: No such thing. My daughters were getting up.

Ricardo: Along with the Mr?

DreamGirl: No mister.

Ricardo: Good to hear. Why the name change?

Maggie wrinkled her nose at the screen. Billie had made the change when they'd returned home from shopping the previous night. The idea had sounded outrageous, but from the moment Maggie had signed on, men began sending messages and wanting to talk to her. Or maybe it was the profile that described her as "blonde, curvy--and fun." It was true, but only to a point.

As hometown, Billie had put "somewhere in Southern California." Also true enough, but it neglected to mention they were at least one hundred miles from the Los Angeles suburbs and miles from anything resembling a city.

Billie had taken it all in stride. "No one's honest on here," she'd said with a shrug. "It's a game." The game hadn't stop there. Her friend had brought over a disk with a picture of a pretty blonde woman with the curves promised in Maggie's profile. "If anyone asks for a picture, send that. It's my cousin Sheila. She's a model, and she said I could use it. No one needs to know what you look like. That could be dangerous."

The thought of being that devious would never occur to Maggie, and she doubted she would ever use it. False pictures, descriptions that bordered on dishonesty, names to attract attention--it all seemed so fake, so unreal. When Billie had claimed the computer was nothing more than a virtual world where people could live out their dreams and fantasies, Maggie had questioned what she was doing. Then she'd gotten involved in a conversation with someone nice, and concerns about Billie's lies had lessened.

A clanging outside drew her attention, and Maggie turned to peer out through a lacy curtain. Tools littered the driveway. Jack was back under the car again. What was he doing to the thing? Billie had told her the brake job should take a couple of hours, but he was working on it for the third straight day. The girls were still in bed, but he had been back under the car as soon as the sun came up. All she could see were long, tanned legs, bare below his shorts.

Leaning over, Maggie pushed back the curtain a few inches to peek out. Her pulse surged sharply and her breathing quickened at the sight of the muscles flexing as he moved. The room grew hot and close, despite an overhead fan, and Maggie waved her hand in front of her face to get some air. Sunlight glinted off the fine hairs of his well-developed calves. To have lived so long next to such a hunk still shocked her. Maggie let out a long sigh and let the lacy curtain drop. This needed to stop.

She'd never paid attention to men before. The Air Force had some very good looking guys in their ranks, and she'd never given them much beyond a cursory look when they came into the store. Maggie was as pleasant to the young, handsome men as she was to the balding, pot-bellied grandfathers.

"Okay," she whispered, her breathing still uneven. Maggie fanned her face with her hand more rapidly. "Enough of that."

Her attention returned to the computer. Billie had demonstrated how to call up a profile of a person online so now Maggie called up Ricardo's to see who he was. There was none.

> *DreamGirl: How come you have no profile?*
> *Ricardo: Ack! Somebody stole it!*
> *DreamGirl: No kidding?*
> *Ricardo: I reported it. Cyber police expect to find*
> *the culprit any day.*

This guy had a good sense of humor. Another screen popped up. *LuckyDog* wanted to talk to her.

"Aren't you the popular one?" she said with a giggle.

Maggie checked two lists of names she'd been keeping. One was a secret list of men with whom she'd enjoyed talking. The other was a list she would never talk with again. *LuckyDog* was not on either list. After jamming her lists back into her drawer, she sent him a quick message saying she would get back to him. Her fingers were getting faster on the keyboard.

Deception might be wrong, but Billie's name change did more than bring her male attention. Maggie couldn't remember the last time she'd had so many men flirting with her--not just talking, like the guys down at the store--but flattering her for her wit and quickness. Most unusual was that instead of feeling shy or embarrassed, Maggie found it easy to type in sassy, clever answers.

There was something about sitting safely in her home in her robe and pajamas, knowing no one knew where she was or what she looked like. At least today she wore a new green satin robe and matching nylon gown complete with lacy ruffles, courtesy of their trip to Los Angeles. Billie had selected it. Still, no one knew what she looked like or who she was. Maybe Billie was right. In this virtual world, Maggie could talk to anyone on an equal level. She was not plain old Maggie with the big hips and thick glasses. She was blonde, curvy *DreamGirl* with the cute quips. She thought of a good answer for Ricardo and typed it.

>*DreamGirl: Did you offer a reward? Missing: One Profile.*
>
>*Ricardo: I'll let the cyber cops find it. They promised a quick arrest. Do you think they would lie?*
>
>*DreamGirl: I've heard computer cops spend all their time in the virtual donut shop.*
>
>*Ricardo: Don't tell me you're a skeptic? I like to believe in the goodness of mankind.*
>
>*DreamGirl: Actually so do I. You might call me a cock-eyed optimist.*
>
>*Ricardo: Well, so am I. I just worry someone is out there misusing my profile.*

Maggie smiled at the screen. She was pleased she had sought Ricardo out again. He seemed rather nice and down to earth.

>*Ricardo: I have a secret. A deep, dark secret.*
>
>*DreamGirl: Tell me. I promise I won't spread it around to more than ten or twenty people.*
>
>*Ricardo: Take notes then! I only give it once.*
>
>*DreamGirl: Fire away. Not only am I an optimist, I can be trusted.*
>
>*Ricardo: Okay, the secret is I'm a nice guy. Not many people know that.*

The comment wasn't unusual. Many of the men who chatted with her said they were nice guys wanting to talk to someone interesting. Perhaps some of them were like her, worried about their looks or too shy to speak in public. Having to deal daily with strangers, Maggie forced herself not to be shy or afraid to talk, but at times, she still recalled the painful shyness of her teen years. She could understand lonely men who simply wanted good conversation, but couldn't do it in person.

She typed a response for Ricardo.

DreamGirl: That's what they all say.

Ricardo: Of course. But remember one of them is a profile thief.

DreamGirl: How could I forget? And just so you know, I am a nice woman here.

Ricardo: No one would tell you they are bad.

DreamGirl: I don't know about that. Some men on here like bad girls.

Ricardo: Not me. I like sweet, nice, cock-eyed optimists. I bet you are pretty too.

DreamGirl: How would you know?

Ricardo: Well, you certainly type pretty!

Maggie laughed as a loud rapping sounded on the back door. She jumped and leaned sideways to look into the kitchen. Jack stood in the doorway. He wiped sweat from his forehead with the back of a large hand, staining it with a long stripe of grease. As he lifted his other hand, she saw a bright red streak of blood.

"Are you all right?" she asked, lurching to her feet.

"I cut myself on the jack," he said with a grimace.

"Oh! Come in."

Feeling slightly guilty at playing computer games while Jack labored, Maggie told Ricardo she had to go and signed off. She pushed her chair away from the table and hopped to her feet as Jack stepped inside. His hand was wrapped in a dirty rag, and blood seeped from around the edges.

Having dealt for thirteen years with unpredictable accidents, Maggie moved forward with purpose. She gestured him toward her. Taking his hand, she removed the rag and walked with him to the sink. She flicked on the faucet and began running cold water over the cut to clean it. The gash across the back of his hand was not so big that it would require stitches, but it looked painful and blood continued to ooze from the wound. After washing it, she placed a clean towel on it and held it tightly.

"Hold that on there like that," she ordered, pressing his other hand down on the towel. "It'll slow the bleeding. I'll get the first aid kit."

She turned to the door, but at that moment April came into the kitchen, blinking sleep from her eyes.

"Oh, good. April, bring me the first aid kit from the bathroom," Maggie ordered crisply.

~ * ~

Her smooth efficiency didn't surprise Jack. He'd seen Maggie operate in a crisis before. Like when May fell off her bike and broke her leg. Or when April tripped while hopping over a patch of cactus. Or when a dozen customers with screaming children all wanted snow cones drawn at the same time the gas islands were busy with customers waiting for the pumps to be cleared.

That wasn't what got his attention. It was her, Maggie. She smelled fresh and clean, like jasmine or lavender. He couldn't help but notice the new emerald green robe that turned her creamy skin more lustrous than normal. It even brought out the honey color of her hair. Unfettered, it flew in small, appealing ringlets around her face. He thought about the night he had touched it and how soft it had been. It looked that way now, as though it would be soft as strands of dancing silk.

Maggie's hands were cool and gentle on him, and goose bumps broke out on his sweaty skin. He could imagine what a sight he made with sweat dampening the middle of his grease-stained t-shirt. He smelled of perspiration and oil, but she didn't seem to mind. Her head stayed bowed, examining the wound to see if the bleeding had stopped.

"What are you doing with that car?" she asked. "You've been busy with it for more than two days."

"I noticed it needed an oil change, so I did that, and your shocks were going out, so I've been working on them."

Her head flew up and behind the thick glasses, her chocolate eyes grew wide. Panic filled them and her voice rose a notch. "How much is that going to cost?"

He tried to reassure her with a quick smile and obvious wink. "Don't worry, I'm saving you money. I was able to get the cost down by buying the whole works all at once at a bargain price at the base store."

She heaved a sigh of relief. "I appreciate that."

April hopped into the kitchen carrying a compact, red tin box. She put the box on the counter and flipped it open. It held an assortment of bandages, gauze, tape, a tube of antibacterial ointment, bottles of pills and other small items.

"You look well stocked," Jack teased.

"You can never be too prepared when you have two teenagers," she admitted with a weary smile.

April shook her head and rolled her eyes, a picture of teenage attitude as she rested her hand on a tilted hip. "Oh, Mom, when was the last time we needed that?"

"Last week," Maggie reminded her. "When you skinned your knee."

"That was just a scratch."

Her hand touched the sleeve of Maggie's robe. "I love this robe. It's so soft. Did you touch that, Jack? It's satin."

"I'll get blood or grease on it," he said ruefully. He would like to touch it. Or maybe do more than touch it. Like pushing it more open across her soft skin with one finger. But as he was thinking about that and gazing down at the tempting site of creamy neck, a stinging pain lashed his hand.

Reflexively he jerked away, but she held his hand tightly.

"You just stay still," she ordered, nimble hands cleaning the cut with whatever it was that stung like a bee. "That will only burn for a minute."

Jack didn't want to move. He was enjoying watching her work, stopping every so often to push up her glasses. She finished with the cleaning, applied some sort of ointment and then expertly wrapped gauze around his hand. She sealed it with tape, which she cut off with her very white teeth.

"I'm not sure if you want to go right back to work. And you should probably see about getting a tetanus shot," she warned.

He smiled at her concern. "Sure, Mom," he said playfully.

Her head tilted up to him, surprise written on her face as her eyes grew big and brown behind her thick glasses.

"Have you ever thought of getting contacts?" he asked without thinking. It was a thought that had come to him when they were in the casino and he kept watching her shove her glasses up her nose.

She blinked, her eyes looking even larger. "Contacts?" Her voice filled with surprise as though the thought had never occurred to her.

"Never mind. Just thinking off the top of my head."

"It's a good idea, Mom," April said behind her. The teenager was digging through the cabinets pulling out dishes and utensils, and banging them on the counter. "You want to stay for breakfast, Jack?" she asked. "I was going to fix French toast."

"I might be convinced," he said. "I just bought a big jug of fresh orange juice. I doubt I'll finish it before it goes bad," he offered.

He checked for Maggie's reaction, but she was busy re-packing the first aid kit. Perhaps he shouldn't have made the comment about contacts. From the way she joked about her weight and eyesight, he knew she was sensitive about them.

And who was he to be saying anything? His gaze lowered to his dirty t-shirt and wrinkled shorts. He looked horrible and smelled worse. He looked at Maggie, with her shiny new robe. "Why don't I go home and clean up a bit, and I'll be right back?"

~ * ~

Maggie helped April with her breakfast fixings, but her mind was still on Jack. Her heart had been pounding erratically the whole time she worked on his hand. She'd never noticed how well-formed and capable his hands were. Even the small things about him were catching her attention now. Like the warm, masculine scent that rose from him, the very shape of his well-developed forearm. She knew he had a desk job at the base, but the muscular definition of his body spoke of a man who worked to keep himself in physical shape. She knew about his daily running, but did he work out at the base as well?

The whole time she'd worked on his hand, Maggie had felt his eyes on the top of her head. She'd had to totally focus on the job at hand to keep her fingers from trembling. This had to end before she made a fool of herself. Forcing her thoughts from Jack, she let her gaze wander back to the computer screen, which had changed to a crazy geometrically patterned screen saver.

The computer buzzed, and at this hour, it was probably filled with people from all over the country talking. It was like a party she'd been invited to attend, and now it was going on without her. But going to that party was preferable to thinking about her handsome next-door neighbor.

Maggie concentrated on getting out eggs, milk and bread for the French toast. May made an appearance, but seeing April and Maggie busy in the kitchen, she retreated to the computer in the other room.

April began beating the eggs with a whisk, silky hair falling in her face.

Maggie reached over and tugged at April's blonde hair, which was uneven and split at the ends. She pulled it back behind her daughter's ear. "I should trim this. Or maybe we should get it cut. Elma's has a special going on, and we can afford it right now."

April yanked her head away. "Mom," she said, drawing out her name. "I'm growing it out."

Of course. She should have guessed. April was always doing something new. At least May kept her thick hair cut short and close around her face.

"Well, put it in a pony tail or something. It looks sloppy, falling in your face like that."

"You're a fine one to be talking about sloppy," April grumbled, looking up from her mixing bowl.

"Now what does that mean?" Maggie asked, a slight pang of hurt running through her..

April's teenage eyes were impolitely blunt. "Look at Cassie. She's never had a boyfriend in her life, but she found a husband."

"Is that what you want? For me to go husband-hunting?" Shock stiffened her spine. Over the years the girls tried their hand at matchmaking from time to time, but Maggie also had made it clear to them from the time they were small that she thought their father was coming back. They had always known about the picture of Al that she kept in the bottom of a trunk by her bed.

Before April could answer, Jack came through the back door. His gaze went from her to April as though he knew they were in the middle of a discussion. He had cleaned up and changed into a fresh gray t-shirt and faded jeans. His black hair was neatly combed, like he was going someplace special and not simply coming next door for breakfast. In his good hand, he carried a plastic bottle of orange juice. It was the fresh-squeezed type, she noticed. He held up an unopened package of bacon in his bandaged hand.

"Did I miss anything?" he asked as Maggie pulled a frying pan out of the bottom of the stove.

Taking the bacon from his hand, Maggie murmured a quick thanks, shooting a warning glance at April as she walked by her. The teenager simply smiled back mischievously.

"I was just telling Mom she needs to buy more new clothes than a bathrobe and lacy nightgown," she said. "We spent a ton of money yesterday, and that was all she got. It's not like anyone is ever going to see the nightgown."

Maggie's cheeks burned and she avoided Jack's eyes as she poured him a cup of coffee. She could feel his eyes on her as she placed the coffee on the counter next to him and retreated to the stove. "I think the neighbors see me in my bathrobe more than anything else. Between feeding Kayla in the morning because you've forgotten and getting the paper, I feel like I'm outside in it all the time." She began placing pieces of bacon in a frying pan.

"Maybe," April said, "but it would be nice to see you in a dress sometimes."

"Did someone say something?" Maggie asked, looking over at April in surprise. The comment did not sound like something even her outspoken daughter might volunteer.

"Grandma did," April blurted. "She wanted us to make certain you got a dress yesterday, and then you didn't do it."

"Well, I'll talk to Grandma," Maggie replied, feeling slightly hurt. She glanced at Jack. He was acting as though he was not paying attention to the conversation as he stirred sugar into his coffee. His eyes met hers across the room. Maggie wanted to ask him what he thought, but decided the question was too personal. Best they drop that sort of talk.

His eyes went to her robe, and suddenly she grew warm all over, even inside. The sight of his large masculine presence made the kitchen seem even smaller than its normal cramped quarters. And she was suddenly aware of the intimacy of his being there while she was still in her robe and nightgown.

Maggie turned down the flame on the bacon. "Could one of you watch this while I go get dressed?" she said.

"Are you going to put on a dress?" Jack said, a boyish grin slashing his face.

Maggie's teeth clenched and her cheeks grew hot. "I only own one dress," she admitted, throwing a murderous look at April.

Her daughter gazed innocently back at her. "See?" she said, as though proving her point.

Maggie sighed unhappily. "Okay, I'll think about it." She didn't check to see Jack's reaction as she walked to the hall.

~ * ~

A peaceful quiet rested on Cactus Bluffs, with only the cheerful chirps of crickets filling the night. Occasionally, the roar of a car speeding through town drowned out their song. Jack glanced down at Maggie as they walked across the lawn toward his house. He was leaving in a couple of days, and he wanted her to have his keys to water his fish and plants.

Her head tilted back, exposing a length of creamy skin. In the gloom of the back porch light, he could see she was looking up, studying the dark, cloudless sky bejeweled with stars.

"That's the constellation Gemini," she offered, pointing at the sky, outlining it with a finger. "I always look for it. The Twins, you know."

"Right. And over there is Leo," he told her, his finger moving across the sky to a familiar outline.

"You know the stars?" she asked in surprise.

"I studied them when I first got stationed here. There's no better place to see the stars than in the desert. No lights to get in the way. Orion is barely visible on the horizon. Can you see it? It's usually overhead in the morning when I run just before the sun comes up."

She laughed, a full throaty sound. "I've always wanted to study the stars, and this week I've been doing that online."

"Oh, really, and I thought all you were doing was flirting around like Billie," he teased.

He knew she had been spending a lot of time on the computer in the evening. In the past he could see the reflection of her television set through the lacy curtains in the window. Lately the only light that stayed on in the evening was the lamp in the corner of the family room, the lamp near the computer.

This week, when he had been watching the girls until midnight, he'd gotten up at six to go out on his run before the heat of the day settled in and found that lamp still on. Was she studying the stars all night?

"I'm sorry I won't be here next time you have to work late," he said.

"Well, my folks will help out. They've already agreed. Besides you shouldn't worry about us. You'll be off in the desert with your war games."

Every year the military gathered in the desert for simulated combat. They would be gone for five weeks, and normally he liked the Spartan nature of it. This year he hated leaving. He had to admit part of it was because he had been spending more time with Maggie and the girls. For the past week, she'd come home and had dinner with them before returning for the late shift at the store.

"This is my last time for the games," he mentioned as they walked through the fence to his yard.

Maggie had been staring up at the stars, and she stopped walking. "Why?"

"I'm retiring at the end of my hitch."

"You're leaving?" she asked, and he could have sworn she not only sounded shocked, she sounded disappointed.

"Well, yes." He resumed his walk across the grass and she fell into step beside him.

"Where will you go?" she asked, after a moment of silence. "Back to Washington? Is that where you're from? It's funny. As long as we've been neighbors, I've never known where you came from originally."

"New Mexico," he admitted. "A small town in northern New Mexico. It's only a little bigger than Cactus Bluffs, but my folks are still there, one of my brothers, too. It's near the mountains, not too far from Taos. Very pretty country up there. That's probably where I'm going when I get out. I may buy a little restaurant. At least that's what I've been thinking."

"A restaurant?" Surprise entered her voice.

"I thought you knew I was a cook before I came here. I don't mind being a communications officer. It's preferable to working in a hot kitchen here in the desert, but I've always enjoyed cooking."

"I didn't know that."

"Maybe I'll cook for you and the girls sometime," he offered. "I don't like to do it just for myself."

Her face turned up to him, lips slightly parted. Her nod was swift, and he heard a quick intake of breath.

Jack studied her in the dim glow from his front porch light as they reached his house. The light of the moon turned her skin golden. Even her sandy hair appeared lighter. As usual he wanted to touch it and for an instant he almost did. Instead he cleared his throat and fumbled in his pocket for his keys.

He pushed the door open, gestured for her to enter, and she stepped inside. The lamp, on a timer, cast a dim light in one corner of the living room.

"We're going to miss you, even for a couple of weeks," she said, looking around the small house.

He thought about how it might look to her, seeing it through her eyes. Jack's house was about the same as hers, though it seemed larger since he had less furniture and fewer personal belongings. He'd repainted the inside all white, pulled up the old carpets and laid down new wooden flooring. The rich woodwork in the archway that separated the living from dining rooms was stripped and revarnished. Even the old cabinets in the kitchen had been repainted a gleaming white. He'd furnished the living room with only a few pieces of Swedish modern furniture, preferring to use up one wall for his entertainment system. His second bedroom served as a home gym since he never had out-of-town guests. State-of-the-art rowing equipment and free weights helped him keep in shape.

His aquarium took up part of the wall in the dining room, where he'd also set up his office area, much like Maggie. As they walked into the house, she followed him to the long, rectangular tank. It gurgled, a dim light casting a glow against the blue green pebbles on the bottom of the tank. An array of fish slowly drifted by the front. Leaning over, Jack showed Maggie where he kept the food in a cabinet under the tank. He demonstrated what she would need to do to keep the tank clean. The twins had requested the job--for pay, of course--but he knew better. Obedient and well mannered as Maggie had brought them up to be, both could turn into recalcitrant teens when they felt like it. He constantly fed Kayla because they forgot. He didn't want to take that sort of chance with his valuable fish.

"I love your fish," Maggie said, studying them, eyes intent on the darting fish. "So many varieties. What's that striped one? I can never remember."

"It's called a loach. See those? I just bought some new Black Mollies, and the loaches like to chase them. I may have to separate them before I leave. And keep an eye on the Angel fish. They can be pretty finicky."

They were very close to the tank and she lifted a finger toward it. Without thinking he caught her hand. A bolt of electric awareness shot up his arm, sending fire racing through his veins.

She turned to him, her eyes very wide, confusion filling them. His heart was pounding, thudding so rapidly, he feared she could hear it in the stillness of the house. A pink tongue snaked out of her lips, moistening them, making them shimmer in the glow of the fish tank.

Alarm bells sounded in his head, and Jack found himself leaning toward her very pink, very plump lips. As he moved, the light reflected behind her and he saw Carla's picture, almost as though it was watching him.

Jack dropped her hand and pulled back quickly. He cleared his throat and turned away. "There is extra food in the kitchen," he said, gesturing toward the dark doorway. It was in the same place as hers.

Her head dropped, and she nodded mutely. Had she realized he'd nearly kissed her? He feared she did. Her cheeks were a soft shade of pink, and her chest below a white striped shirt heaved slightly as though her breathing rate was elevated.

Jack ignored the enticing view and walked into the kitchen and flipped on the light. She followed closely behind him. Again, he could feel her eyes going around the room. She had never spent much time in his house. The girls had come by often when they'd been using his computer, but Maggie never had. Clean and simple was how he'd describe it. He opened the door of a cabinet and pointed out the extra boxes of fish food.

"Now, besides the fish, there are two plants in the living room, one in the bedroom and the one by my desk," he explained. "All they need is water, and once a week is probably enough. Oh, and if you want to use the spices I've been growing in my spice garden, go ahead." He pointed to a small row of plants that lined a window sill.

"You grow your own spices?" she asked in amazement.

He shrugged, forcing a smile across his lips as embarrassment overwhelmed him. The guys at the base would never let him forget it, if they knew, so he'd never admitted it to anyone. "I told you I like to cook, and I've always felt fresh spices make things taste better."

Maggie walked over to the length of plants, studying them as she had the stars earlier. A small finger touched one of the tender basil leaves. "Maybe I'll check that out, though I don't really cook much. The girls prefer hamburgers and pizza."

"Try the fresh basil on their next pizza," he suggested, but she was shaking her head.

"I don't think they'd appreciate it, but maybe I will."

"Well, that's about it," he said, taking his extra set of keys off a peg by the back door. He handed them to her and offered to walk her back to her house. Discomfort remained from his moments with her next to the fish tank, but letting her walk home alone at one in the morning was wrong. He couldn't allow that. When she started to refuse, he insisted.

Their walk was silent, and he found himself looking down at her. She didn't reach his shoulder, and the moon cast a shimmer onto her curly hair.

"If you need to use my car, feel free," he told her as they reached her house. "It's the least I can do since you're taking care of the house."

"No, that's fine. Since you got my car fixed, it's running great."

"Okay." He lingered, realizing he didn't want to leave. He would not see her again for weeks, and the thought bothered him more than he wanted to admit.

Maggie's face was aimed up again at the sky, studying the constellations.

"I used to count the stars when I was a little girl," she said softly.

"And now you don't because you're busy learning about them on the computer," he teased lightly.

She laughed, a rich sound that sent a strange tremor through him. "I guess."

"Well, I'll let you go. Just don't stay online all night."

"Who said I'm staying online all night?" she said, her voice becoming a little hard.

"Don't get all upset." He didn't want to mention a possible search for Al again, so he teased her in a different direction. "I just figure you're looking to find someone like Cassie did."

"I am not!" she protested. "I just like talking to people. What's wrong with that?"

He didn't like the defensive feeling that came over him. Or was it protective? Or maybe even jealousy at the thought of her conversing with strange men? He tried to keep his tone light.

"Nothing I guess, but I don't think it's the romantic answer to your dreams. That's fantasy."

"I know," she said, but her face had gone shuttered and closed. "I'd better go in. Good night, Jack. I hope your war games go well."

Before he could apologize more fully, she was gone.

~ * ~

How did Jack know she was spending so much time on the computer? Maybe Billie had told him. Or the girls. But what difference did it make? Or was there more to his comment? She thought about their moments near his fish tank. Had he meant to kiss her? For a minute, it had seemed like a possibility. Maggie had even felt his breath on her face. But could that be possible? She rubbed her fingers over newly sensitive lips as she sat at the computer keyboard. Why hadn't he?

Then reality stepped in, squashing her crazy notions. Of course he wasn't thinking of kissing her. Why would he want to kiss plain, pudgy Maggie? Who would want her? That's probably what he meant when he talked about fantasies. Her glance fell to the keyboard. Some of those guys online seemed to want her. They were always ready to flirt with *DreamGirl.*

They didn't know what she looked like, but that didn't matter. Not online. Maggie looked down at her hips. For once they didn't seem as big. Actually, she had lost a couple of pounds in the past week since getting the computer. Often she came home and got online during the time she had once snacked. It was hard to eat potato chips or candy bars at the keyboard. Both had the tendency to turn her fingers greasy. If she got hungry, she found herself turning to apples or carrot sticks. They didn't get into the keyboard.

She turned on her computer and signed on, telling herself that the rejection from Jack didn't matter. He might not think she was interesting or pretty enough to kiss, but others did. She had never imagined talking so freely to men she didn't know, but she was doing it regularly online.

Maggie had always been friendly with anyone who came into the store to buy cookies and gas, but the thought of flirting with unknown men had terrified her. Now she could carry on teasing, almost suggestive conversations. On the computer, she was *DreamGirl,* the belle of the ball, someone a man wanted to get to know. She had never dreamed of having so much attention from so many different men, but it was coming to her nightly.

A mirror across the room caught her reflection. Suddenly she was no longer overweight Maggie, with the limp, lank hair and coke-bottle glasses, wearing faded jeans and a frayed blouse, living in a cramped bungalow filled with used furniture, its walls decorated with bargains from the town's thrift shop.

No, when she signed online, she was *DreamGirl* with flowing, golden hair, wearing a cranberry silk gown that covered a sleek figure and shimmered when she walked, head held high and regal. She could picture herself floating down a gleaming circular staircase in a marble-floored mansion to greet her many beaus who sat waiting in a parlor filled with antiques, real Oriental rugs and oil paintings by the Masters.

<h1 align="center">*Six*</h1>

"You're going to do what?" Billie asked, her hands poised over the hot dog grill. She was cleaning it prior to starting to grill the morning's first offerings. Dick required a thorough cleaning at the beginning of every shift. It was a chore neither enjoyed, so they took turns.

The store smelled of coffee and fresh cinnamon rolls that had arrived only moments earlier, a special delivery from Sarah's Bakery down the block. If they didn't sell out in the first hour--which they usually did--Maggie would eat one at her morning break. But this morning, her mind was far from the delectable scent of cinnamon rolls. Billie stopped cleaning, and frowned at Maggie, waiting for her answer.

Outside, a car pulled into a pump. Maggie crossed to the register, ready to clear the pump. Luckily, the man used a credit card, so it didn't require any effort on her part. She had chosen to tell Billie about her plan early in the day. Before long, a crowd would fill the store as Cactus Bluffs' working people headed off for their jobs, stopping first at the store to get coffee or cinnamon rolls. Once the daily flow of traffic began, the store would be too busy to talk.

Maggie turned away from the register and faced Billie, who had resumed cleaning. Her red hair bounced as she rubbed the grill vigorously, thin lips pressing together in what Maggie knew was a look of disapproval.

"I said, I've decided to meet this man I've been talking to online in person. Didn't you say you had done that yourself?"

Billie stared at Maggie incredulously, her head turning slowly from side to side. "Not after only a couple of weeks. That's crazy. You don't even know this guy."

"Sure, I do," Maggie protested defensively. "His name is Bob and I've been talking to him online almost every night for the past month--not just a couple of weeks. He's a nice guy from Albuquerque, and he wants to meet me in person." She knew the exact night he'd started talking to her online--the night after Jack left--four weeks ago.

"He's not coming here!" Again a note of shock flooded Billie's voice.

"No, I couldn't do that," Maggie admitted with a shake of her head. "Not in this town. There would be too much gossip. He wants me to meet him while he's in Las Vegas on a business trip. I'm thinking of going this weekend."

"Maggie, since when did you suddenly start going out with men?" Billie asked, giving up on cleaning the grill. She tossed aside her cleaning rag, walked over to the counter and stood across from Maggie, hands on her hips. Her pencil-thin eyebrows drew together and her blue eyes were filled with concern. "I've tried for ages to set you up with people and you always say no."

"It's not like I'm going out. I'm simply meeting this guy. And I have let you set me up from time to time," Maggie reminded her, turning away and pretending to stack snack cakes into a more orderly display. She had not dated much as a teenager, and she did not go out now unless her friend set her up. Heck, she couldn't remember the last time anyone had asked her for a date.

Besides, this wasn't a date, she kept telling herself. She was meeting a friend. The computer made the difference. The men she talked with online were unlike the men Billie tried to set up as blind dates. At least these men enjoyed her wit. Bobcat, Ricardo and GreyWolf all told her they appreciated a woman who liked to make conversation. When Maggie went out with Billie, she got the impression the men were in search of immediate sexual gratification. No one wanted to get to know the real Maggie.

"What about your car?" Billie asked. "Will it make it?"

"Jack said I could take his car anywhere I wanted."

Billie gasped, her eyes growing wide. Again, she began jerking her head back and forth in censure. "I don't think he meant Vegas. That's a two-hundred mile trip."

"He won't mind." Maggie turned away, thinking of Jack as she had been for the past few weeks. It had never occurred to her that she might miss him, but she did. He was due back next week and a sudden bout of giddiness rushed through her at the thought of seeing his handsome face.

Caring for his fish had turned out to be an easy chore, but Maggie would prefer to have him back. She liked having him next door in case of emergencies, and the truth was she missed seeing his smiling face as he worked on his lawn, or his quick waves as she headed off to work. Or maybe watching him in his shorts and tank top as he returned from his runs? She shook her head quickly. She shouldn't be thinking about him.

Thinking about meeting Bob was preferable. With Bob--online-- she could be witty and clever, something she could never be around Jack. And sometimes she imagined that Bob might be handsome and hunky like Jack. Maybe that was why she'd gotten so carried away with talking to him so quickly. Maybe that was why she wanted so badly to meet him in person.

She turned back to Billie.

"Do you want to go with me? As a former jackpot winner at the Golden Gulch, the hotel sent me an offer for a free room for the weekend of my choice."

"I would love to go," Billie said. "But I can't. I lost too much money last time we were there. I wasn't the big winner," she teased, elbowing Maggie playfully in the ribs.

"I guess I can go alone." Maggie hadn't been certain she wanted Billie to go, but she had to make the effort to invite her.

"Just don't meet this guy alone the first time," Billie warned, gazing at Maggie with open concern. "Don't run up to his hotel room, or invite him to yours. That's dangerous."

"I am not that stupid," Maggie said forcefully. "I just want to meet him."

"Do it in public," Billie urged.

"That was what I was planning," Maggie admitted. "A hotel bar or coffee shop. Gee, Billie give me some credit."

"Do you want me to keep the girls?" Billie asked.

"I was going to leave them at Mom's. They're happier at home, but I don't have anyone to watch them there."

"They hate being at your mother's. Do you want me to stay at the house? I don't have any hot plans for the next couple of days, and it would be a fun distraction."

"Would you? They'd love that. You can sleep in my room, and after the girls go to bed, you'll have the computer all to yourself." Maggie was pleased by Billie's offer. She had not dared ask her friend, but it was exactly what she'd hoped would happen. "May I ask one favor?"

"Sure," Billie said.

"Don't tell the girls what I'm doing. They'll tease me or expect too much."

Billie gazed at her, eyes filled with doubt. "Okay. And I hope you meet your Prince Charming or win a big jackpot, but I want your promise that you'll keep in constant touch."

"Yes, worry wart," Maggie said, sticking her tongue out at Billie. "But I doubt I'll meet my Prince Charming or win another big jackpot."

~ * ~

The shiver of anticipation surprised Jack as he briskly stepped up to Maggie's back door. He had missed her, and found himself looking forward to seeing her smile. He must be anxious. Otherwise why rush over the instant he'd showered and changed after being dropped off?

For the past several weeks he'd been worried about her. Jack had almost written her a letter or tried to make a call to her. His cell phone didn't work in the desert, but he'd considered making the call from a command tent. He had finally decided against it. What reason could he give for the call? To ask about his fish?

It seemed too personal to write a letter detailing his activities, and she would probably think he was crazy. Why would she care what he was doing in the desert anyway? She had her own life and her daughters to keep her busy.

May opened the door, her young face lighting up in a bright, welcoming smile when she saw him.

"Jack, you're back," she said, pushing open the door. Kayla squirmed beside her and he leaned over to ruffle the dog's fur. She shoved by May, nearly knocking her down and lunged into the yard.

"I thought I'd come by and see how things were going," he said, trying not to make it obvious that he was looking beyond her for Maggie. He had read her work schedule on the refrigerator door. She was supposed to be on an early shift this week, which meant she should be home. Her car was in the driveway.

"I thought you weren't coming back 'til next week. At least that's what Mom said."

"That was the plan, but my unit finished up early. Is your Mom around? I wanted to thank her for taking care of the fish. The house is spotless, so I know she must have done some dusting." He tried to look beyond her again.

"Actually, no." May shifted, looking suddenly uncomfortable. Her eyes slid past him to his garage, and her face turned slightly pink.

Something stirred inside him, like a knot tightening in his stomach. "Is something wrong?"

"Oh, no," she said quickly, attempting to smile. "But she's…" May took a deep breath, tilting her head down. Her eyes avoided his, and her thin fingers fidgeted with the door knob. She studied it as though it was the most intricate thing in the world. "Don't get angry, okay, but she drove your car to Las Vegas. I'm sure she meant to tell you when she got back."

A quick knot of tension formed in his middle section. He wasn't angry as much as he was concerned. He would rather think of her driving his air-conditioned SUV than attempting to cross the desert in the heat in her own car. He hadn't had a chance to work on the radiator or change the hoses, and some of them looked like they needed fixing. Still, traffic from Los Angeles to Las Vegas on the weekend could clog the narrow road, and she wasn't used to such driving conditions.

"That's fine. I told her she could use it. So she and Billie are doing the town again?" He attempted a laugh, but it came out forced.

Again she fidgeted with the door knob. "She went alone."

"Alone?" Shock ran through him. Maggie didn't strike him as the sort of person who would want to do Las Vegas alone.

Her eyes flickered and found his as though she understood his surprise. "I know. Can you believe it? I think there's more to it. You might ask Billie. She's staying with us, but she's still at work."

His lips tightened. What could have possessed Maggie to drive to Las Vegas alone? Did she hope to win another jackpot? Certainly she was too levelheaded to suddenly get caught up in the thought that because she'd won once, she might win again so quickly. He knew some of the guys at the base thought that way, but the levelheaded Maggie he knew was not a compulsive gambler.

Despite the blistering afternoon heat, he jogged over to the store. Teenagers just out of school packed the tables by the snack bar. A line of customers snaked away from the front counter. Picking up a bottle of cold water, Jack drank it as he waited in line to pay for it.

By the time he got to the counter, the store was nearly empty. Only one or two teens were still drinking sodas at the tables across the store.

He put down the nearly empty bottle and added a candy bar to it.

"Hi, Billie. I was looking for Maggie," he said.

She turned away from him, walking over to busy herself with placing fresh wieners into the grilling machine. She closed it before giving him her attention.

"Oh, she went to Las Vegas," she said with a wave of her hand as though Maggie might have just gone across the street instead of attempting a two-hundred mile trip across the desert--alone. She stepped up to the register and rang up his purchases.

"So May told me," he said impatiently, shoving a bill across the counter. "I wondered why she would go alone."

Billie put down his change and leaned across the counter toward him before speaking in a low voice. "I told her not to take your car. I understand if you're angry with her."

"But why didn't you go with her? There's something you're not telling me."

Billie's eyes followed the teen customers out the door and then she turned to him. "I told her not to do this, either."

"Which is?" He was about to pop across the counter, yank her across it and shake her.

She looked away. "Okay, she went to Las Vegas to meet someone she's been talking to on the internet."

"What?" His voice was like a cracking whip and she looked up at him, her blue eyes startled.

"I told her it was a stupid thing to do."

"Damn stupid," he said. Sudden visions of Maggie with some burly man who wouldn't take no for an answer surged into his head. Or maybe her being held close by someone and enjoying it. "Why the hell didn't you stop her?"

"She's a grown woman," she began but he turned and lurched away. Some of the guys had told him on the ride home that they were planning a trip to Las Vegas this weekend. Maybe he could still grab a ride.

~ * ~

Maggie sat on a barstool, kicking her crossed leg at the air, nerves on edge. Light glittered off the glasses over the bar across from her and onto the slick surface of the video poker game at her fingertips. Absently she punched the buttons, and the cards electronically flipped over. Nothing. Her fingers pushed the button again.

She glanced toward the main casino floor. The Rags to Riches machines blinked and sang their familiar tune to the players sitting in front of them. She would rather be one of those players, putting in her nickels and hoping for another major jackpot.

Her eyes swept across the glittering lights of the main casino floor. A steady crowd flowed through the aisles. Older women with gray hair jingled their plastic buckets as they searched for the next machine. Young women wearing short skirts and impossibly high sandals scanned the crowd for men while absently placing coins in the machines. Young men in torn t-shirts jostled each other as they looked for the nearest cocktail waitress. Tourists with golden tans in neat shorts and straw hats limped across the gaudy carpet as though they'd spent too much time walking in the hot sun. They all seemed to have somewhere to go. Across the casino, a loud yell rose from the Roulette table, while in another corner, the long line for the buffet snaked across the outer edges.

Was this the dumbest thing she had ever done? Why hadn't she let Billie talk her out of it? It was a good thing that Billie had promised not to tell the twins. They would fear their mother was going crazy. Maggie doubted her sanity herself. She had never done anything like this. She feared that everyone who walked by knew what she was there to do.

Even worse, she had not been entirely honest with Bobcat about her looks. She had never admitted that the picture she'd sent him was someone else. In a moment of weakness, Maggie had sent him the picture of Billie's cousin. He said looks were not important so hopefully he would not mind one small act of dishonesty.

Still, Maggie knew she looked different than normal. She smoothed down her blue cotton granny dress. Its crispness felt good against her skin. Its small pink flowers complimented her fair skin and its princess cut slimmed her chunky figure. The v-neck displayed just a hint of cleavage. It was the first new dress she had bought in years. All she needed for work were jeans, striped uniform shirts and red vests. For church, she normally wore blouses or sweaters and skirts.

Her face and hair had undergone changes, too. Billie had trimmed her hair and let her borrow hot rollers, so her normal ringlets were gone. Upon arriving in Las Vegas, Maggie had carefully curled it to make it hang in becoming waves that framed her face. She even wore make-up. What would he think? Would he accept her as she was?

Maggie shoved her glasses up on her nose. There was nothing she could do about the glasses. Her eyes were bad, and she could not afford contacts. If she took off the glasses, she would be stumbling around and might not even see him.

She glanced around the room again. Her eyes picked out a slim man with thinning dark hair and black horn-rimmed glasses. He was rail thin and short, not at all the description of Bobcat in the computer, who had described himself as tall and muscular. Still this man wore a pink carnation in his lapel and carried a single rose, which was how they said they would recognize each other. Maggie had a gardenia sitting on the bar beside her. She picked it up and twirled it, just in case.

As the man grew closer, he looked toward her. His eyes went past her and then back. He seemed to notice the flower. He smiled slightly, displaying crooked teeth and nodded toward her. Yes, it was Bobcat. She smiled back and slid off the barstool. He pulled out a chair at a small round table as Maggie approached.

"Hi, Bobcat?" she asked, tension running through her. This was worse than being a teenager on a first date. Talking on the computer was easy, but this was difficult. What could she say? All her witty comments from the computer vanished from her head, as though they'd all been stored inside the electronic machine.

"Hello. Actually my real name is Bob," he said, and his eyes openly surveyed her ample figure.

Disappointment swept through Maggie at his open appraisal. The smile was still on his face, but it was no longer as wide, and it did not extend to his blue green eyes.

He wasn't exactly good looking himself. His face was thin, his nose long, and unless she was wrong, he wore a toupee. His hair was receding, and a few gray strands at the temples poked through very black hair that looked fake. He wore a brown polyester shirt, open at the collar and a blazer too big for his slight frame. His brown pants were wrinkled, and grease stained one leg. They sat down and he beckoned a waitress.

"That's some costume," he told the young woman, his eyes sliding over her low cut top and nipped in waist. The skirt barely covered the thin woman's backside, and every time she bent over, its minimal cut displayed the firm round lines of her bottom through shimmery black hose.

"Sure is." The woman's voice was bored as she put down napkins. She wore very thick make up, and her vivid red hair looked less natural than Billie's, but Bob was staring at the waitress as though she was a chocolate sundae. She ignored him.

"What'll it be, dearie?" she asked Maggie.

Maggie glanced over at Bob. They had teased each other about ordering drinks with umbrellas, but he ordered a bourbon on the rocks. Disappointed, Maggie ordered a gin and tonic.

"What about you?" he asked the waitress. "Can I get you something?"

The waitress glanced at Maggie and back at Bob. "No, can't drink on the job," she said before turning around and flouncing off. Bob's eyes followed her as she swayed across the room.

An uneasy silence cloaked the table as Maggie and Bob traded glances.

"You look different than I expected." Bob's gaze slid away, looking around the room as though he wanted to avoid her eyes. "If it wasn't for the flower, I would never have found you."

"The flower helped me with you, too." Maggie proudly held hers up. "I don't think I would have recognized you, either."

"I guess we both look different." He gave her a sideways glance, a frown furrowing his brow.

"I never expected to meet you when I first started chatting with you," Maggie said, attempting a smile.

"Well, here we are." His voice was cool.

The waitress arrived with the drinks. "Shall I run a tab?"

Bob nodded and gave the waitress a sly smile that was beginning to irritate Maggie. He was supposed to be here to meet her, not flirt with someone else. "Are you here all night?" he asked the woman.

"For another hour," she said.

"Maybe I'll hang around." He punctuated the comment with a wink.

The waitress shook her head, her voice steely. "My boyfriend's picking me up."

His rude behavior might have bothered Maggie more but she was beginning to wonder if it wasn't her fault. After all, she had sent him the false picture.

"I hope you're not angry at me?" Maggie asked, attempting a smile before taking a small sip from her drink.

"Why would I be mad?" His eyes refused to meet hers, remaining instead on the waitress as she bent over another table.

"Because I don't look like my picture?" She adopted her most apologetic tone. "I guess you realize now it was fake."

"No big deal. People do that all the time. I guess you're cute in your own way." He gave her a cool smile.

"You're older than I expected," she pointed out, as though his lie matched hers. Up close, she could see wrinkles around his eyes and mouth. "I didn't mean to fudge."

He shrugged, eyes on his drink. "There's a lesson there. But it doesn't matter. Everyone does it."

Maggie shifted, discomfort flooding her. "I've learned my lesson. I'll be more honest in the future." She forced a laugh and tried to smile, but none of it came off.

He downed his drink in a big gulp and nodded. "Well, as long as we're here, we might as will make the best of our time."

"Okay." Relief surged through Maggie. If he could forgive her, she would forgive him. "We'll have fun. Do you gamble?"

"I wasn't thinking about gambling, Maggie," he said forcefully.

"You weren't?" Maggie asked in surprise. Going to dinner might be nice. She'd never been to a nice place for dinner except when her folks took her to nearby Los Angeles suburbs for her birthday. Or maybe they could go to a show. She and Billie had talked about doing that.

"I have a room over at the Easy 8 Lodge," he said with a sly grin and a wink that set her skin crawling. "I figure we can have some real fun. If you know what I mean?"

Maggie was so shocked she almost choked on her drink. Was this what Bob wanted all along when he asked to meet her?

She shook her head. "I don't think so, Bob. I came here to meet you, and that's all. If you had something else in mind, then you're out of line."

"I see." His dark face reddened, and his thin lips turned down into a scowl.

Maggie backed off her anger. "Please don't misunderstand. I want to get to know you. I thought that was what you wanted."

"Sure." He attempted a smile, but it didn't quite make it. He lifted his drink, noticed it was empty and pushed back his chair. "Excuse me. I'll be right back."

Maggie nodded, pleased at the interruption. Perhaps they could start over when he came back. They could talk for a while and then decide if they wanted to go to dinner. He certainly was different in person than he had been online. Where were all those witty comments and the sly teasing flattery? Did he think she was here for sex? Hadn't he understood she was interested in friendship only?

Maggie glanced at her watch. Ten minutes had passed, and Bob was not back. She waited another ten minutes before the truth dawned on her like a slap across the face. Bob wasn't coming back. As she downed the rest of her drink, Maggie saw the unpaid check on the table. Not only had she been deserted, she'd been stuck paying the tab.

~ * ~

Jack almost missed her. The thick glasses gave her away. Everything else was different. Her curly ringlets were missing, and her sandy hair fell in flattering curls to her shoulders. Her cheeks were thinner, giving her face a nice oval shape he'd never noticed before. They were every bit as peachy perfect, but the color was different. Rouge dotted them, the faint outline visible. Her well formed lips were painted even larger by a garish shade of red lipstick. Light blue eye shadow covered her eyelids and black eyeliner and mascara outlined her brown eyes behind the thick glasses. The make-up was jarring, but so was the rest. Her dress looked new and clung to her in a becoming way that sent the male alarms in his head to clanging. It's low-cut neck displayed lots of creamy colored skin.

Damn! Maggie had changed. Or maybe he was just taking note of how curvy her figure was for the first time. He hadn't seen her in four weeks, after all. The swells of her breasts rose and fell in a rhythm that threatened to hypnotize him. For a crazy moment, he fantasized about what they would look like below the lines of the dress.

She sat at one of the slot machines where she had won the money last time they'd been in town. He'd called Billie to find out where Maggie would be. Billie had actually sounded pleased that he was coming.

Maybe he was being foolish. Who was he to say about whom she could or could not meet? She was his neighbor, his friend, another part of his brain argued. He couldn't just abandon her when she was doing something stupid. He'd do the same for his kid sister.

Her face was pale, morose and unless he was wrong, Maggie was on the verge of tears. Maybe she'd lost her money. Or maybe the man she'd come to meet had stood her up? The thought of why she was in Las Vegas rekindled the anger that had driven him to hitch a ride with some of the guys coming to Las Vegas for the weekend. He marched over to her.

"What the hell do you think you're doing?"

Startled brown eyes flashed up at him, and she pushed her glasses up her nose as though she couldn't believe he was standing in front of her. Color flooded her falsely pink cheeks, and fresh tears pooled in her large brown eyes behind the thick lenses. Before Jack knew what was happening, Maggie thrust herself to her feet, hurled her body at his chest and began to sob.

Seven

Neon lights flashed from every direction, the false light casting colorful, changing images across Maggie's honey-colored hair. The night air along the Las Vegas Strip was balmy, a slight breeze cooling sidewalks still hot from hundred-degree heat during the day. Bumper-to-bumper traffic clogged the thoroughfare, turning a stream of cars into desert tortoises. Jack and Maggie walked along the crowded sidewalk on a constant collision course with an ever-shifting mass of humanity.

Families with scampering children competed for room with lovers holding hands and looking like they were headed for the nearest wedding chapel. Slightly inebriated groups staggered along carrying beer bottles and large drinks with long straws. Wide-eyed tourists with cameras at the ready brought the surging mass to lurching stops from time to time.

Jack glanced down at Maggie. Her cheeks were clean now, eye shadow and mascara only faint memories. She'd washed off all her make-up after she'd stopped crying. A good portion of it remained on his pale blue cotton shirt.

He'd cleaned some of it off while she'd washed her face, but he doubted the shirt would ever be free of the black mascara or red lipstick.

Maggie turned toward him, as though she knew what he was thinking, and her full lips puckered into a frown. "I'm sorry for messing up your shirt. I'll wash it when we get home. Maybe I can get out that make-up. I have to do it all the time on April and May's clothes. They're going through an experimenting phase."

"Don't worry about it," he said.

She shoved her hair out of her face, anchoring it behind one ear. Her expression was glum. "You must think I'm a nut."

Jack still wasn't certain what he thought about Maggie's plan, but he could see she was earnest in her question, and his answer mattered. "No."

"Billie told you what I was doing."

"Yes. And I agree with her, it was stupid."

Her face flushed again and her brow furrowed into a frown. "I know. He wasn't even nice."

The acknowledgment that she actually met the man rocked Jack like a stinging slap to the face. "You met him?" he asked incredulously. "I thought he stood you up."

"It would have been better if he did. Then it wouldn't have cost me fifteen dollars for drinks."

"Cost you? He made you pay?"

Her face grew somber, hurt and for an instant he wanted to touch her solemn cheek. "I guess he didn't like my looks, so he just left me sitting there with the check. Stupid old Maggie. It took me half an hour before I realized he wasn't coming back."

She pressed her lips together, and Jack feared she was going to cry again. A passing tourist who had his camera focused on the pirate ship behind them smacked into her shoulder and Maggie murmured an apology, stepping around him. Suddenly Jack wanted to do something nice for her, something to cheer her up.

"I take it you didn't have dinner..." he began.

Her hair danced on her shoulder as she shook her head. "All I ate were some peanuts on the bar. Not that I need to eat," she said, patting her hip.

Jack stifled the urge to protest. She looked as though she had lost a few pounds, but he'd never liked the way she brought attention to her ripe figure. He actually found her curves appealing, though he reminded himself he shouldn't be thinking of her body.

"Let's go to dinner," he offered. "We can find a restaurant that isn't one of those low-dollar steak joints we went to last time and have a nice dinner."

Maggie stopped walking, forcing a shift in the surging crowd. Someone behind him collided with Jack. A short barrel of a man in shorts muttered an expletive as he moved past them. Jack offered a quick apology and turned to Maggie.

She was gazing up at him with wide, disbelieving eyes. "Really? Dinner at some nice place?"

Her look was so appealing, Jack was driven to take it a step farther. "Sure. Maybe later we could even go to a show."

Her breath rushed out and the brown eyes grew wide behind her thick glasses. An unbelieving smile wreathed her face. "Could we? I'd love that. I wanted to do it last time, but I didn't have money. I have it now, but I... I didn't want to go alone."

He waved off her concern. "I'll go with you, and it'll my treat for taking care of the fish. You did a nice job."

Her smile dissolved like shifting sand. "I took your car."

"It needed the drive. It only goes from my house to the base. Cars need a good long drive every so often."

"You're being very nice to me," she said solemnly.

Maggie's contrite look was filled with such sincerity, he almost laughed. His earlier anger had dissipated into concern. What had brought her here to do such a crazy thing? Jack always thought of Maggie as a very cautious person. This current behavior didn't fit his neighbor.

From out of the crowd, a hand caught his arm. A young woman with long, pale blonde hair in a very short, latex skirt and tank top that ended short of her middle stood before him. "Hi, baby, want to party?"

He resisted the urge to jerk free, but instead slowly pulled his arm away from her. "I'm… uh…" He turned to Maggie and took her arm. As usual when he touched her, his senses all went on alert. "…occupied," he finished.

Her gaze slid to Maggie, as though seeing her for the first time. "Oh, sorry," she said and moved on, swinging her hips in an exaggerated fashion.

"Sorry about that," he said, looking down at Maggie, concerned the encounter might disturb her.

She dropped her head and pressed her lips together, repressing a smile. "It's okay. I guess she thought you were… on the town?"

"I don't know what she thought," he said. "She must not have noticed you were with me."

"It doesn't surprise me." Her look of glee lessened. "Most people don't notice me."

"Why not?" he asked. "You look very pretty in that dress."

Her cheeks turned crimson as she murmured her thanks, but behind her glasses, her brown eyes danced, or maybe it was the reflection of the electronic volcano that was beginning to send off streams of light down the block from them. They'd made a point of seeing it when they'd visited the first time, and he didn't feel like forcing his way into the crowd that flowed along the street.

The crush pushed him toward Maggie, and Jack leaned closer to her, inhaling a sweet floral scent, like honeysuckle on a warm summer night. As he linked their arms, she inhaled sharply. For an instant, he feared she might pull away, but instead, she stepped closer to him.

"This way no one will question if I'm with someone, and you won't get lost in that crowd," he said as though that might better explain his action. "Where would you like to go for dinner? Steak? Italian? Chinese?"

"Some place French," she said, tilting back her head to smile up at him. "I've always wanted to go to a French restaurant."

"French, it is then," he said, glancing at his watch. "Though I don't know where we're going to get in at eight on a Friday night."

"There's a French restaurant back at the hotel," she said, fumbling for something in her bag. "I have special consideration because of my jackpot win. Actually, I looked at the menu and it looked great." Her voice was becoming more animated.

"You don't want to go some place in one of the big hotels?"

"No, this restaurant had things like frog legs and Steak Diane. And escargot. Have you ever had escargot?"

Jack found himself smiling at her open enthusiasm. He hadn't been to a nice restaurant in years and as they walked back to the hotel, he realized he missed special nights. He and Carla had always enjoyed dining out and made a point of going to a different place nearly every week. He pushed thoughts of Carla away. This was not a night to become depressed with thoughts of losing her.

~ * ~

Maggie's heart thudded against her chest as Jack helped her push her chair to the table. She told herself the reaction was due to the new experience, not because she was so aware of her tall companion's vibrant masculinity as he hovered over her. The maitre d', a small, thin man in a black tuxedo, handed her a leather-bound menu that was so heavy, she nearly dropped it through her shaking fingers. He picked up a linen napkin from the table and leaned toward her. Maggie flinched as though he was about to hit her with it before realizing he simply wanted to put it on her lap.

When he was gone, she let her gaze travel around the stately, darkened room, her breath catching in her throat. "I've never been to a place like this," she admitted in a hushed voice. Her palms were damp as she pushed them across the napkin on her lap.

Everything about the place suggested elegance. Each table was covered in a snowy linen tablecloth and had its own flickering candle in a glass bowl. The upper half of the walls were covered with what looked like deep, green tapestry. The bottom was a rich, dark wood paneling. The carpet was thick and lush beneath her feet, and Maggie was tempted to slip off her sandals to see if she could sink her toes into it. Crystal glasses gleamed in the candlelight and the intimidating assortment of polished silver in front of her glowed.

Maggie hazarded a look at Jack, who appeared quite at home, despite the elegance. She pressed her lips together, trying to partially stifle the smile that threatened to crack her face, she was so happy. He was studying a smaller menu.

"Would you like wine?" he asked.

"If you would," she said. Maggie had never been much of a wine drinker, but the idea of wine went with the restaurant. She tried not to let her gaze wander around the room like the country bumpkin she feared she resembled. Did people eat in places like this all the time?

Jack set aside the menu and smiled across the table at her, his eyes gleaming in the candlelight like azure amulets. Her heart resumed its racing level. He had never looked more handsome. He'd changed when they'd returned to her hotel, putting on a pale periwinkle dress shirt, tie and navy blazer. Maggie didn't know he had such clothes and she didn't ask why they were in his suitcase.

The jacket emphasized the size of his large shoulders, and she thought of how they looked when she saw him in a tight t-shirt or even a tank top when he ran. Maggie's cheek grew warm at the thought and, fearing her face might give away her thoughts, she buried her face behind the large leather menu.

The long, detailed menu written in script was a mystery to her. Words like *crepes* or *soufflé*, she knew. *Coq Au Vin, Bourguignon,* and *Amandine* were unknown.

"What do you think?" Jack asked.

Still behind the menu, she pushed up her glasses and shook her head. "This isn't exactly Chin Lee's Gourmet Palace. No chow mein or wonton soup in sight."

His chuckle was throaty and sent trembles through her insides. "But you wanted escargot?"

"Yes. Snails. That's what Billie told me to try. She said they're delicious." Actually the escargot was another unknown to her except for Billie's description. Maggie had no idea what they looked like, much less how they might taste. The waiter approached and thankfully Jack ordered only the escargot and asked him to return.

Maggie was at a loss for what to order for the rest of the meal. She fidgeted with the menu until Jack volunteered to help. She'd have to remember that in case she ever really did have a date. Either go to an Italian, Chinese or Mexican restaurant where she'd have a chance of recognizing one or two items on the menu or learn more about this French stuff.

When she told him she wanted fish, he found sole, which he said came in an almond cream sauce. He chose Consommé for soup and a house salad which again carried lots of ingredients that were a mystery to her.

Maggie could feel him watching her and guessed his curiosity about her would-be date, but she would rather not let him know what had happened with Bob. The less said about that, the better.

The escargot arrived, six shells in a silver vessel that looked like a poacher. She squeezed the implement that came with the snails, recalling a scene from the movie *Pretty Woman* where Julia Roberts flung her snail shell. Determined not to let that happen, she listened intently as Jack explained how to pick up the snail, hold it in the implement and then extract the meat with a delicate silver fork.

The process was tricky and Maggie feared she was going to end up like Julia Roberts, flinging the slippery little shell across the room, but she managed to get out the meat. The texture and taste surprised her. Her nose wrinkled as she slid the delicacy around in her mouth.

"It's like rubber, lots of garlic," she said, shaking her head.

"Try it with some of the bread," he offered, pushing the heavenly smelling warm, fresh rolls across at her.

She extracted the next one and put it on a piece of French bread. She lifted it to her lips again and again her face twisted. "May be I'm not meant to be an escargot fan," she said, putting down the bread.

"Well, don't worry about it. I can finish them. I've always been a fan. Would you like another appetizer? Like a plain shrimp cocktail?"

"I'll make due with dinner. And maybe later, dessert?" She knew what *Crepes Suzette, chocolate torte* and *Crème Brule* were.

Jack's eyes grew soft, the edges crinkling as he smiled at her. "Whatever you want. It's your evening."

A dream evening, Maggie would have told him and that was what it was like. The sole was buttery, its sauce rich, and it melted on her tongue. The potatoes that accompanied it were swimming in a creamy sauce unlike anything she'd ever tasted.

Maybe it was the Chardonnay they drank with dinner or maybe it was those watchful eyes that she could feel on her the whole time, but Maggie had never felt so alive. She giggled at the silliest things. As she looked around the room with its tasteful decor and the other patrons in sequined gowns, men in sport coats and a few even in tuxedos, she was amazed that she was here. Plain old Maggie Hemple. Surrounded by such splendor. It wasn't like she had never dreamed of such things, but Maggie had always figured if she did this, it would be with Al.

She forced him from her thoughts. So often, she envisioned him with her in different situations, playing with the girls, driving in the desert. Tonight, she could not imagine a better companion than Jack. She had no idea what they talked about--the girls, his time in the desert during the war games, the guys he worked with at the base, a couple of crazy customers at the store--but it all seemed to make sense.

By the time they finished their very tasty dinner, they were both full and decided desert could wait. In the hotel lobby, Jack checked and found they could get into a late show.

Maggie was amazed. Dinner and a show? She couldn't be more pleased. She had never been a big dance fan, but the extravaganza they attended was part acrobatics, part dance and all glitz. Maggie's mouth dropped in wonder as tall dancers in very high sandals sashayed onto the stage in skimpy, sequined costumes and colorful, oversized headdresses that looked ready to topple off their heads at any second.

"This is unbelievable," she gushed in a breathless tone, her hand touching his arm. A major buzz raced across her skin, sending off enough voltage to light the neon signs around the stage. Did he notice that, or was he totally unaffected by it?

"I'm pleased you're enjoying it," he said with a warm smile.

"I've seen the ads, but the colors, the costumes. Wow! And the dancers, did you see how precise they were?"

The dancers surprised her more with their ability to keep their big headdresses from falling as they strutted around the stage. Her favorite part of the show, though, was the acrobatic maneuvering of several small Chinese performers. Even Jack seemed to enjoy that.

As they left the theater, he looked toward the coffee shop, but Maggie was still too full for desert. Fearing he was going to suggest they call it a night, she turned toward the lounge, where country music poured from large speakers. He seemed to notice the direction of her gaze.

"Shall we go have a drink?" he suggested, "or would you prefer desert?"

The lounge was more inviting. "Could we have a desert drink?" she asked.

"Chocolate martinis it is," he said, gesturing her toward the lounge.

Maggie felt like she was soaring on the smoke-filled air, a seagull suspended in midair. She'd never had such a wonderful time in her life. The French dinner in a dim restaurant lit only by candlelight, the glitzy show, now drinks in a Las Vegas lounge that offered a live band. It was like a date. Too bad this was not real.

As they sat down, the band leader announced a break, to her disappointment. When the short-skirted waitress came over, Maggie inwardly shuddered. Thoughts went back to the way Bob had inspected the cocktail waitress in a skimpy outfit earlier, but Jack didn't even look up. His eyes were on Maggie. A tremor rippled through her insides and goose bumps rose on her skin. What would it be like to be on a real date with Jack?

~ * ~

The restaurant didn't offer chocolate martinis, so they opted for brandy and coffee. Jack found he couldn't take his eyes off Maggie. Had he ever seen her so alive? Well, maybe, when she was playing Frisbee out on the lawn with the girls. But watching her wide-eyed reactions to everything around her had been an eye-opening experience. Her excited gaze circled the lounge as though she was memorizing the place. Maybe she was filing it away to remember later. She seemed to have such grand curiosity about life, but it seemed to him she kept herself removed from it. Why didn't she ever just let herself go and enjoy life?

He'd been making small discoveries about her all evening. He'd found her enthusiasm fun to watch as she'd surveyed the menu in the restaurant, turning over the French words, trying to pronounce them. He was no whiz at French himself, but he'd heard them before. They had sounded new and fresh rolling off her inexpert tongue.

Even though she hadn't enjoyed the escargot, that had been a fun experience, too. She had studied him intently as he'd explained the right way to eat them and then had eagerly tried to extract the buttery snail.

At the show, her soft brown eyes had lit up at the fantastic, sequined dance costumes and the elaborate headdresses, twinkling as bright as the lights that flashed around them.

When their drinks came, he found he needed to ask the question that had been plaguing him all night. What had driven her to travel to Las Vegas to meet that stranger?

"Did you really want to meet someone new?" he continued.

The smile froze on her face, and she lifted one shoulder in a shrug. Her face lowered so that her eyes could not meet his. A fingertip outlined the grain of the false wood on the table top.

"I guess," she said in a small voice.

"If you want to go out with someone, why don't you ever try the men closer to home?"

"No one would want to go out with me. At least not the nice men." Her voice was sad, resigned, and her red nails tapped at the side of her coffee cup. He had a feeling they were as false as the table top. He'd never seen her nails anything but short and blunt.

"Of course they would," he disputed. "Sometimes I think it's like Billie says. You put them off."

"Maybe. But I figure…" she stopped.

"What?"

"Well," she said, her tongue flicking out to moisten her lips. "I've known most of the men in town since I was young, and most of them know me or my story."

He swished the brandy around in the snifter, thinking about the dark night they'd searched for Kayla, when she had related her story to him. He took a sip of his drink, savoring the taste on his tongue, feeling the red hot burn as it slid down his throat.

"I don't see why something that happened more than thirteen years ago should make a difference now," he said quietly.

Her eyes studied the polished table top as though it might hold the answer, while her fingers fidgeted with the frames on her thick glasses. "I don't know. I guess it's the small town atmosphere."

"Maybe. Does everyone know the whole story?" he asked. "I mean, you told me some of it, the basics..." His voice trailed off. He wasn't certain what he wanted to know.

Maggie licked her lips, still studying the table and then began to speak in a low, almost inaudible voice.

"You know most of it. I was seventeen and like so many silly girls, I was hoping to get the attention of a young flier. In those days, the town was always busy, not just with people passing through. Cactus Bluffs was bustling with young airmen, pilots. Maybe I watched *An Officer and a Gentleman* one too many times." Maggie smiled ruefully at the recollection. She sipped at her brandy, her face wrinkling as she swallowed the drink.

"How did you meet him?" he prompted.

"I was working part time at the store. Al came in for gas and stayed to flirt. We were inseparable from that day on, up until he left. I couldn't imagine life without him. I was devastated. I waited day after day for a letter from him. But there was nothing. When the twins were born, I half expected to wake up and find him standing at my bedside."

Her voice was sad, quiet. Jack disliked Al Williams without knowing him. "And you've never heard a word all these years?"

"No." She took a deep breath, hands cupping the snifter. They appeared to be shaking. He wanted to reach over and touch her, but something in her somber, set face stopped him.

"It must have been rough, having the twins alone."

A sad smile turned up the corners of her lips. "Yes, but I wouldn't trade my girls for anything. That was the only good part." Her eyes lifted to meet his, and they began to sparkle. Maybe it was the reflection of the candle in the center of the table, but an inner fire burned in her copper eyes. "I don't regret choosing to have them. He left me with some money--that I could have paid for a doctor..." She stopped, took a deep breath and then continued.

"My parents were appalled but surprisingly supportive. They helped me a lot. Working part time at the store until the girls were born, I was able to support myself. They bought that house and let me live in it virtually rent free. The rest of the town wasn't as charitable. Everyone knew what had happened to me. So, while I wasn't exactly a pariah once the twins were born, I wasn't befriended by the other girls."

"So except for your parents, you were pretty much alone? What about Billie?"

"I didn't know Billie very well then, and it wasn't just the girls in town. Once I was on my own with my babies, men decided I was... well... easy. But I wasn't. I gave myself to Al because I was in love with him. I wasn't going to turn into... well... you know... just to please them."

Jack sympathized with her story. He could imagine what it must have been like for her, waiting for the twins to be born, waiting for the man who had never returned. And she'd had to endured it all under the watchful eye of her small-town neighbors with their small-town ideas and prejudices.

"Did you ever try to reach him?" he asked.

"My Dad did when the girls were three. He wanted Al to contribute support. Al was out of the service by then, and we couldn't find him."

"I'm sorry."

Maggie attempted a smile, but tears glistened in her eyes, and Jack almost regretted asking her about why she had made the attempt to meet someone new. He could understand her feelings of desperation.

"Now the girls are growing up, and there hasn't been any excitement in Cactus Bluffs in years. The town is as dry and dusty as the land around it, and sometimes I feel like my life is that way, too."

"Do you think about leaving?" he asked.

"Sometimes. But then, how would Al find me if he wanted to?"

The comment hit Jack harder than he would have liked. He hated to remind her that if Al really wanted to find her, he could have come back a long time ago.

The band was returning and kicked into a song. They fell into silence. He studied Maggie as they listened to the music. Surely she didn't think Al was coming back, did she? She had made her comments so hopefully that he knew part of her really did think that Al would return. She swayed in time to the music, whispering a few words from the song. A few couples got up to dance, and she watched them wistfully. Jack waited until the song ended and then as a new one began, he vaulted to his feet.

"What do you say we dance?" he invited.

Maggie blinked, surprise on her face, her eyes growing wide as saucers behind her glasses. "You want to dance with me?"

"Sure. I feel like moving," he said, twisting his shoulders and holding out both hands.

Uncertainly, Maggie got to her feet and moved toward him. He took hold of both her hands and pulled her forward to the floor. He folded her to him, her soft curves pressing against him. He had not been this close to a feminine body in years, and his male senses leaped to life. A small flame of desire smoldered in his veins. Her hand was small in his, trembling slightly as he folded it against his chest. Jack leaned over and deeply inhaled the clean floral scent of her hair. His chin brushed it. Her hair was soft as silk against his skin, and the flame flickered higher and hotter.

Jack's heart began to thump, and he wondered if she could hear it, or perhaps notice the uneven level of his breath. He forced his breathing to a regular pace. The dance was heavenly, but it sent his blood racing to the boiling point.

The dance ended too quickly and yet not quickly enough. Jack enjoyed the feel of her in his arms and the way her palm rested on his upper arm, the feel of her soft curves against his body.

When it was over, Jack knew he could not chance another one. He was being unfair to Maggie. And to Carla. And himself. Maggie still wanted Al to come back. And their few missteps reminded him how much he missed the fluid dances he had once shared with Carla.

As they sat at the table again, Jack found he could not look at Maggie. He feared being overcome by her smile or hypnotized by those warm, brown eyes.

"Do you think Al will come back?" he asked, taking a drink of tepid coffee. His brandy was gone, but he wasn't about to order another. Too much brandy and wine would definitely put his self control in trouble.

"I've always thought he would. Billie thinks I should just get over him. The idea of loving only one man is silly according to her. But I can't think of it any other way. Can you?"

Carla popped into his mind. Until that moment, Jack had always believed the same thing. He would never love anyone the way he had loved his wife. Jack couldn't imagine feeling that strongly for anyone, but there was more to his belief than thinking only one woman could capture his heart. Loving someone else might also mean the sort of pain he felt when he lost Carla. He didn't want the happiness, if it was followed by the pain.

And he doubted anyone could ever be like her.

He shook his head. "No," he said tightly.

To his relief, Maggie shoved her chair back and got to her feet. "We should go. It's very late, and I'm tired."

Jack inhaled sharply and tossed bills on the table for the check. He was more than ready to call it a night. They walked in silence to her room. He waited while she fidgeted in her purse, looking for her room key.

As he started to say goodnight, Maggie caught his arm, sending off strange, electric sensations. She reached up suddenly and kissed his cheek, her warm body pressing to him for just a second. Still it sent a vibrant thrill through him, re-igniting the fire he had managed to douse before they'd left the lounge.

"Thank you for tonight," she whispered and as she pulled back, he found himself studying her very pink lips. What would it be like to taste those lips? To have her for just one night?

Then his eyes met hers. Eyes filled with wonder and questions. No, Maggie would never give herself to any man but the one she loved. And he was never coming back.

Jack mumbled good night and turned and walked away, his chest filled with what? Pain? Desire? Regret? The worst thing was he didn't know.

Eight

When Maggie woke in the morning, she found herself with the same thought that had lulled her to sleep. *Jack!* They would be driving back together that morning, and she ached to see him.

But, her more practical side questioned, what good would it do? Jack wasn't going to be interested in her, not the way Maggie might want. He would never see her as anything more than his pudgy neighbor. He might go out of his way to help her, or even make her feel good as he had the previous night when he had taken her out to dinner, but that was as far as this craziness was going. Did she want it to go farther? The thought frightened and yet at the same time excited her.

Maggie knew she would never forgot those special moments at dinner, when he'd taught her to eat escargot. Or their dance when his hard arms had wrapped around her, holding her to his well-muscled chest. She had been tempted to lay her cheek against that chest, just to see what it would feel like, but had held back, enjoying instead his warm, masculine scent and the gentle touch of his hand on hers. He'd gripped her hand so lightly and yet it might have been an electrode sending electric pulses through her blood.

His other palm had pressed to her back, scorching her skin through the thin cotton material of her dress. Her insides had come alive, and her lower body had tingled with strange sensations, womanly sensations.

But that was wrong. Hoping for more from him was wrong. Comments about his wife told her how he felt. Much as Maggie believed there was only one man for her, he obviously felt the same about his dead wife. He would never want anyone else, and she understood his feelings.

Dancing with Jack had been magical, though she had fears about her rusty dancing skills. She hadn't done much dancing over the years, except with her father or brother at weddings or birthday celebrations. She wouldn't have expected Jack to be much of a dancer, but he surprised her with his grace. He was a smooth dancer and good at leading. Luckily, she'd only stepped on his toes once, well, maybe twice, but he hadn't seemed to notice.

Maggie showered, running her hands over her bare skin, wondering what it would be like to have him see her like this, to have him or anyone touch her. For once, she felt like a woman, a real woman with physical wants and needs.

She began to dress, studying herself in the mirror as she dried her hair, careful to brush out the curls that took on their own life when she let them dry alone. Knowing the ride across the desert would be hot, Maggie twisted her hair into a knot and anchored it on top of her head.

Was she that bad looking? With make-up the day before, her looks had been better. Maggie Hemple would never be a beauty, but that didn't mean she couldn't look good if she tried. Maggie pulled the new cosmetic bag out of her suitcase and began carefully applying foundation as she had been instructed by Billie.

The unfamiliar stirring Jack had awakened in her had given rise to a new thought. If he could make Maggie feel like that, perhaps someone else could, too. Maybe Al wasn't the only man for her. Maybe Al wasn't coming back. Perhaps the time had come to see if someone else belonged in Maggie's life.

Not Jack, though. She wasn't about to compete with a beautiful ghost.

Maggie was uncertain when they were headed home, so she called Jack's room to see if he wanted to have breakfast first. She smoothed down her new yellow cotton blouse with its tiny flowers as she listened to the phone ring. She'd paired the blouse with vivid yellow culottes, and catching sight of her sunny reflection across the room, Maggie drew her head up. The woman was very different from plain old Maggie Hemple.

Confidence swelled inside her, or as much as it ever had. With her bright clothes, Maggie presented a vision of spring. She told herself she hadn't taken the extra time to fix her face and wear her special new clothes because of Jack. Still, her skin tingled with anticipation.

"Hello?" He sounded groggy.

"It's Maggie." The newfound confidence began to ooze away. Maybe she shouldn't have called him so early. It seemed intrusive, maybe even forward. "I wondered if maybe you wanted to go have breakfast?"

His deep sigh was audible across the phone. Or perhaps it was a yawn. "Uh, I just woke up. I didn't get to bed until late last night... I don't think I could eat right now."

If Maggie needed any reminder that she meant nothing to him, there it was. He had chosen to stay up--alone--and who knew where he had gone or why. Had he met a woman? She could almost imagine him back at the lounge, dancing with one of the skimpily dressed waitresses, or one of the other women who had been there with teased hair, too much make-up and gold lame skirts. A picture arose of them pressing their thin bodies to his granite frame, whispering flirtatious words to him, words that she couldn't even use on the computer.

"Okay," Maggie said, drawing a quick breath, swallowing her disappointment. "Maybe I'll go have breakfast and do some gambling until you're ready to go, okay?"

"That sounds good. I may sleep for another hour. How about if I meet you in the lobby in two and a half hours? Does that sound all right?"

"Sure, take three hours," she offered, a lump forming in her throat and threatening to explode.

"Thanks," he said.

Maggie hung up the phone, biting hard on her lip. Across the room the same mirror that had reflected the vision of spring now showed the tears that shimmered in her eyes.

Well, this wasn't going to get her down. Blinking the tears from her eyes, Maggie resolved to move forward. She packed her bag so she would be ready to leave and then walked down to the casino.

Despite the early hour, gamblers were already gathered at the rows of machines. The familiar slot songs sang out across the casino. She fumbled in her purse for money. A little slip of paper slid out along with a couple of crumpled bills. As Maggie opened the paper, her breath caught. She stared at the number scribbled on a sheet torn from her notepad at home. It belonged to Ricardo, another of her online friends.

He had given Maggie his number and told her if she was ever in Las Vegas to look him up. Maggie had brought the number along, though she had not told him she would be here for the weekend. She'd expected to spend most of her time with Bob. Maggie made a face thinking of her ill-fated meeting with Bob. What a mistake that had been. Should she try again? Were all men like Bob? Or were there some out there like Jack?

The thought made her heart beat faster. Maybe so. What about Ricardo or Rich? What was he like? Should she meet him? Manager of a pancake house, he was divorced and spoke like a gentleman online. For an instant, she was concerned about her looks. Would he be looking for someone pretty? Or would he take her as she was, extra pounds, thick glasses and all?

Bob might not have been impressed by her, but she had a feeling he would have taken her to bed if he'd had the chance. The guy had only one thing on his mind. Rich didn't seem that way.

She crossed to the bank of phones that lined one of the casino walls. With shaking fingers she dialed the number.

"Hello?"

"Rich?"

"Yep. You got him."

"This is Maggie. Dream Girl from the chat room?"

"Hey, good to hear from ya. When are ya comin' to see me?"

"I'm here… now," she sputtered. He didn't sound at all like Bob.

"Well, hot damn, girl. Let's get together. I work a late shift today. How about if I buy you breakfast?"

Pleased by the invitation, Maggie nodded her head eagerly, even though he couldn't see her. "I haven't eaten breakfast, and I'm starved," she admitted.

"Well, let me treat you then. Where are you staying?"

"The Golden Gulch. Right off the Strip?"

"I know where it is. I can meet ya in the coffee shop in half an hour."

"I'll be there. I'm wearing a white blouse with yellow flowers and yellow culottes."

"I'll have on my favorite blue striped shirt. My favorite shirt for my favorite online friend."

Maggie was smiling as she hung up the phone. This might turn out well after all. Maybe she was finally going to meet a nice guy, someone who simply wanted to talk to her. Maybe in the future, she could return to Las Vegas and he would buy her dinner or take her to a show.

Half an hour later, after putting on more make-up and re-tying her hair, Maggie stood near the door to the coffee shop, waiting. A large man with a pronounced belly wearing a blue striped shirt approached. He had thinning hair that he combed forward in an attempt to hide the baldness in front. His eyes swept the area. Could that be Rich?

Disappointment flooded Maggie. His eyes fluttered past her and he checked his watch. He was obviously looking for someone, so she approached him.

"Hello, Rich?"

The big man looked startled as his cool blue eyes swung down and regarded her. Like Bob's, they swept over her openly, but she saw no spark of recognition.

"Who?" he asked in a voice that sounded very much like the blustery voice on the phone.

"I'm Maggie. Dreamgirl." She forced a smile across her lips, one she didn't feel.

His red-rimmed eyes swept beyond her, and he pursed his lips and shook his head.

"Sorry, I'm not Rich," he said. The man took one more look around and then turned and walked in the other direction, as though he had lost interest in food.

Feeling deflated, Maggie stared after him and then resumed her position by the door waiting for Rich. In half an hour she knew Rich wasn't coming. Or maybe he was the man who had denied being her online friend.

Dejected, she entered the coffee shop and found an unoccupied booth. Even though her appetite was gone, she might as well order breakfast. Jack might want to get on the road as soon as he got up. As Maggie finished, she checked her watch. She still had another hour to wait for Jack. Maybe she should call him and see if he might be willing to leave earlier. No, with the mood she was in, she was liable to start crying all over him again. She needed to get some time between her latest rejection and when she saw Jack. In a way, he had rejected her, too.

Leaving the café, Maggie walked around the casino floor. As she passed a Rags to Riches machine, she stopped. Maybe she would play a few rounds. It might take her mind off the debacle with Rick. But was it worth it to try her luck? It seemed to have turned for the worst in the past twenty-four hours.

~ * ~

Jack found Maggie exactly where he expected to--standing beside the Rags to Riches game. In her yellow clothes, she was the picture of sunshine and his jeans exhibited a tightness that hadn't happened from looking at a woman in a very long time.

He wondered when this awareness would end. He wanted to go back to seeing her in her bathrobe, not noticing the way that small curl fell across her forehead, even when she tried to pull it back, as she had today. The rest of her champagne-colored hair was in a knot on top of her head, but the one curl edged around her face in an endearing manner.

His breath quickened and he forced his thoughts away from the physical side of her. She'd awakened these senses in him that had gone to sleep when Carla had died. He didn't want them back. He couldn't afford to let them come back.

"Thinking of milking?" he asked, standing over her.

Her face colored and then her eyes looked up at him in what? Confusion? Pain? What did he see there? Maybe he shouldn't have taken her out the night before. Holding her had been heavenly, but like this morning, it had given him feelings he didn't want to have. Even her simple kiss at the end had been a mistake. That was what had been the biggest problem. He'd wanted her! Physically wanted her for a painful few moments.

"I... I was going to," she said, a trembling smile crossing her lips. "I didn't expect you for a while."

"I couldn't go back to sleep after you called."

Her hand clapped over her mouth. "I'm sorry. I didn't mean to wake you up. I didn't realize you went back out last night."

He shrugged. "I just went walking around the Strip."

Her eyes clouded and Maggie looked down. He had a feeling he knew what she was thinking about--the young woman who had nearly propositioned him as they'd walked the Strip. A couple of women had done the same thing later. He had turned them both down.

"I couldn't sleep," he went on and then at her look of pain, he stopped. That was a stupid thing to say. But he didn't want this to go any other direction. He couldn't think of her as anything other than his neighbor. She was waiting for Al, and he couldn't imagine that anything could ever be like it had been with Carla. To let her even think there might be a chance was a mistake he could not afford to make.

"Are you ready to leave?" she asked, looking toward machine.

"I was thinking of having breakfast. If you're hungry," he offered, almost hoping she'd already eaten. Relief flooded through him as she informed him she had.

"I wanted to play for a bit," she said, her small hand touching the machine.

He thought about how that hand had felt as he'd held it close to him while they had danced. A ribbon of warmth heated his blood as he recalled the soft feel of her body against his. His eyes ran over the stretch of creamy skin right above the neck of her flowered top. A sudden urge to taste it ran through him and he turned away, inhaling sharply. His lower body was on fire; he needed to get away from her.

"Go ahead and play your game. Take your time. We don't want to get too late a start, but I'm in no rush. I'll come looking for you later."

~ * ~

Maggie sat at the machine dejectedly as she watched Jack cross the casino toward the coffee shop. She'd sensed his coolness the instant he'd said hello. His words had been teasing but there had been none of the glee she normally saw in his blue eyes. She'd either crossed the line with her quick kiss the night before, or maybe he'd met someone special when he went out.

She turned back toward the machine. It was probably better to focus on her gambling than on Jack. Absently, she pushed a twenty-dollar bill into the machine. Her fingers paused as she started to select the number of lines she wanted to play. This was a newer machine than the one she had played the last time. The maximum was nine lines, not five.

Two elderly women sat at the machines next to her, laughing and offering each other advice, cheering each other on. Was that what she and Billie would be like in twenty years? Women with blue-gray hair and smudged red lipstick, laughing over their paltry winnings like a couple of cackling hens?

After a couple of spins, one of the women leaned toward Maggie. "You know, dear, you should be playing that game for all the lines. You could have won on your last spin."

Maggie was playing nickels. At five lines, that cost her a quarter a spin. She gave the woman a reluctant smile. "But if I play all the lines, it's almost fifty cents a spin."

"So live a little," the other woman said, waving her hand as though losing the money didn't matter.

Maggie wanted to tell them she had won a jackpot on one of these machines, but she had played maximum then, too. She knew what Billie would say if she was here. What was there to lose? Maggie could afford to gamble fifty dollars. Maybe by the time that was gone, Jack would have finished breakfast.

Jack. There it was again. She didn't want to think about him and his cool behavior. What would he say if she admitted she had tried to meet Rich? Maybe he would try to be nice to her again. Maggie shook her head. She didn't want that. As much fun as she'd had the night before, she couldn't bear the thought of him doing it out of pity.

Feeling unhappy, Maggie punched maximum coins a couple of spins and then stopped. The payoffs weren't happening. She'd lost nearly ten dollars in just a couple of minutes. What was she doing? She went back to betting her usual minimum.

"Have you tried the quarter machines?" one of the old women asked her.

"No."

"They have them over by the outside door," the other woman said. "My daughter says they're looser, you know, they pay more because they're close to the street? The casinos like people to come in, bet a few coins, win and think they're going to hit the big jackpot so they keep playing."

"I've never come here often enough to form any opinions," Maggie admitted. Their constant chattering was beginning to distract her. "Maybe I'll go try them," she said.

After cashing out of her machine, Maggie took her plastic bucket of nickels and exchanged them for quarters. Walking slowly through the casino, she paused outside the coffee shop and glanced in. The top of Jack's dark head was visible in a booth. He must still be eating. She checked her watch. If he had his food, it would probably be half an hour or so before he would be finished and ready to go. He liked to linger over his final cup of coffee.

She was tempted to go in, sit down across from Jack, order coffee and ask what he had done the night before. Why had he gone out? He said he'd merely walked along the Strip. Had he been alone? Or had he met someone, like that forward woman, while he was walking?

Reaching the outer door that led to the sidewalk, Maggie located the twenty-five-cent Rags to Riches machine the two women had mentioned. Maybe it was worth a shot. She slid onto the seat and shoved a twenty dollar bill into the quarter machine. It gobbled it up and rang up eighty credits. Making a face as she did it, Maggie hit the coin select and line buttons. At first she only played one line. To play five lines would be more than a dollar a spin, but she tried it. Nine lines was unthinkable. In only a couple of minutes, she lost the twenty. Perhaps she should stop. Maybe her luck had turned again. It had burst into good fortune here. Maybe it had reversed itself. All the same, she put in the other twenty. It went just as quickly.

Maggie fumbled in her purse and pulled out her final ten dollar bill. She would play this and quit. A lump was forming in her throat and tears stung her eyes. This whole trip, except for her hours with Jack, had been a disaster. The confidence of the woman who had stared at her across the hotel room in the mirror had seeped away.

Both Rich and Bob had made her feel like a loser. Now she was on the verge of losing fifty dollars. She'd never gambled that much money in her life.

Almost imperceptibly, her luck began to turn. Slowly the money begin to build. That emboldened Maggie to where she began to try nine lines every so often. She forced herself not to think of the fact she was spending more than two dollars a spin.

It happened like before. Maggie was only half paying attention when the cows lined up five across. Her first thought was that she got to milk. Then as the machine began to ring, Maggie realized she had again hit a big jackpot. The bucket filled up and overflowed with coins-- to the tune of ten thousand dollars. The amount seemed astronomical. She could only stare at it, not knowing what to do.

"I won!" she cried to no one in particular. Her chest swelled and threatened to burst. To make matters worse, as she looked around, she was alone. No Billie, no Jack. If only Jack could be there with her. Too bad he was taking so long with breakfast.

Like before, the next few minutes were filled with chaos and confusion as the floor manager came over to make the payoff. All around her people were gathering and staring.

Maggie giggled with excitement, enjoying her momentary role in the limelight. Her hands were trembling and she kept shaking her head in disbelief. Strangers walked up to her and congratulated her, hugging her like long lost friends. If only Billie had been there!

Then she looked up. Jack's lanky figure was coming through the crowd, a puzzled look on his face.

Not caring that she might be acting too forward or whether he might have been with another woman the night before, Maggie thrust herself to her feet and launched herself at him.

She threw her arms around him and, without thinking, reached up and kissed him right on the lips.

Nine

Maggie couldn't stop laughing as they packed the car and headed out on the long drive toward home. She didn't know if her giddiness was from the win or that spontaneous kiss. Jack had been too shocked to react, and she had pulled away the instant she'd realized how foolish she was being. But not so quickly that her insides didn't begin to do a strange rhythmic dance of excitement. Maggie disguised the inner physical giddiness with giggles over her win.

"I just can't believe it. Ten thousand dollars!" she cried as they drove away from the hotel.

"What did the girls say? Or did you call them? Do you need to use my phone?" he volunteered.

"I didn't tell the girls yet. They would be in their early Sunday school class by now, and I didn't want to tell them before they went. Can you imagine that? They'd be too excited to keep quiet and they would probably tell Reverend Smith's wife that their mother won all this money playing slot machines."

Maggie laughed at the thought and Jack joined in.

"I want to surprise them," she added. "That way I can see the look on their faces when I show them this cashier's check. I can't believe it. I still haven't spent all that other money."

"What are you going to do with this latest windfall?" Jack asked, smiling across the seat at her.

Maggie fought off a quick shiver of awareness at the sight of the dimple in his lean cheek. "I don't know. I've always liked to dream of all the wonderful things I would get if I had just a little more money, but I'd never ever thought I'd have enough to do… well, almost anything."

His head tilted toward her as though questioning her statement, and it brought her partially under control--but only a little.

"All right," she admitted, waving her hand at him. "I know it's not a million dollars. I can't do unlimited things. Maybe to some people, this isn't much money. But to me… Well, I can think of so many things we need. Things the girls might like…" Maggie bit down on her lip to stop herself. She was rambling on like April on one of her talking binges.

Jack didn't seem to mind. He kept glancing at her as though he found her enthusiasm amusing. "I don't blame you for being excited."

"You don't think I'm being the slightest bit crazy?"

"You're allowed. Not many people win one big jackpot, let alone two. You're doing very well."

"I guess," she said with another giggle.

A car in front of them slammed on the brakes, drawing Jack's attention. His strong hands gripped the steering wheel as his eyes focused on the road. Maggie bit her lip to stop from saying more. She couldn't afford to distract him. They might end up in an accident and her winnings would go to fix his car.

The hour might be early, but a steady stream of cars lined both sides of the Strip. Maggie watched them for a few minutes, but they weren't nearly as interesting as staring at Jack's rugged profile or studying his chiseled features. What had he thought of her two silly overtures? Or was he totally turned off by them? She didn't dare ask. The gestures had surprised her as much as they'd probably embarrassed him.

Maggie turned away, though there was no way she could ignore Jack. His large presence seemed to overwhelm the small space of the SUV. He looked very good this morning in his form-fitting, dark blue polo shirt and jeans that clung to his lean body. His handsome face was drawn for once, and very dark glasses shaded his eyes. In the close confines of the vehicle, she could smell the tangy, familiar scent of his aftershave. After inhaling it at will as they'd danced, she doubted she would ever forget it.

They were silent for a few minutes while Jack concentrated on the stop-and-go traffic. As they entered the freeway, Maggie turned to him. She wanted to say something clever, be as conversational with him as she often was online with total strangers. Unfortunately, the right words didn't come to mind. Why did he make her so tongue tied?

"What would you do if you had that kind of money?" she asked finally. "Would you do what you said before? Open a restaurant?"

His nod was quick, sharp and left no doubt that he'd given the matter a good long consideration. "Actually, that's no longer just a possibility. I've decided that's what I'm going to do when I retire."

"Need an investor?" Maggie teased, giggles bursting from her, though she knew it was an impossibility.

His full lips twitched, and he chuckled, a low, pleasant rumbling sound that sent shivers through her.

"Restaurants are always a tricky business, but my uncle has this place in New Mexico that he's thinking of selling so he can retire. He says I can take it over and expand it if I want."

Jack had told her he would be leaving Cactus Bluffs when he retired, but he hadn't said when that might be.

"When... when is that?" she asked, hoping she didn't sound as nosey as she felt.

"In two months or so."

"Two months? You didn't tell me it was that soon. Two months?" The thought of him leaving in just two months struck her like a sudden blow to her middle.

"Don't tell me you're going to miss me?" he asked, twisting in his seat to glance at her, a broad wink sweeping down one lid.

Maggie's breath caught, and her body went limp. Like with the kiss, her insides turned to mush. Her cheeks burned red hot and she turned to look out toward the desert as they left the glitzy row of casinos behind. In front of them, the freeway stretched across the desolate desert terrain like a black ribbon dotted with cars.

The realization she might never see him again turned her thoughts as bleak as their surroundings. The desert was a pinkish beige wasteland of sand and scraggly sagebrush punctuated by craggy, pointed rock peaks. With Jack gone, her life would be as empty and barren as the desert floor.

Maggie might not want him to go, but she didn't dare reveal her feelings. It wasn't as though she was in love with him. She was a one-man woman, she'd always told herself, and Al was her man.

Tears threatened, and Maggie took out her darkened lenses and clipped them to her glasses. Leaning forward, she fiddled with the radio, fighting out of control emotions. She was aware of Jack watching her as she turned the knob from station to station, finding nothing but static, a couple of talk radio shows and deejays speaking in very rapid Spanish.

"I hope you learned your lesson," he said softly.

"My lesson?" She stopped twisting the knobs and turned down the radio. His glasses were pointed at her, his expression grim.

"Meeting those men you're talking to on the computer?"

Maggie wrinkled her nose. She didn't need any warnings or lectures from him. She was finished with those crazy ideas.

"I don't think I'll do it again. You know what they say. Three strikes and you're out. I'm down to my last strike."

"Two strikes?" he questioned.

Maggie clamped her hand over her mouth. How silly of her. She had not told him about her plan to meet Rich.

"There were two?"

A heavy sigh escaped her and she turned back to the bleak scenery. Might as well be honest. "Yes."

"The first stiffed you with the bill. What happened with the second?" His voice had taken on a hard note.

A lump formed in her throat, and Maggie lifted the water bottle that sat in the cup holder. She took a sip to see if it might clear the dryness that clogged her throat before answering and admitting to Jack that the man had pretended to be someone else once he'd had a look at her.

"I guess he hated my looks so much, he didn't even want to meet me."

Jack didn't reply for a couple of minutes. His chiseled face had grown rigid, and a nerve jumped in his jaw. "You need to stop this craziness."

"I told you, I learned my lesson."

"I don't know what you're trying to prove," he continued. "That you're beautiful, desirable?"

"You don't need to tell me that I'm not!" she cried, hot tears forming in her eyes. "I know I'm not. I just... oh, hell, I have no idea what I was doing."

He drew a deep breath. "That wasn't what I meant. There's nothing wrong with your looks."

"I'm just overweight, nearsighted, and my skin turns bright red if I'm out in the sun too long. I'll never be tanned, long-legged or pretty. But I'm used to being just plain old Maggie. I'll go back to that, okay? That's what I am and that isn't changing."

"Maggie..." he started, and then stopped, shaking his head.

"Al used to say I was pretty. He even said I was beautiful. Of course I was only seventeen, and I hadn't had two babies." She stopped her tirade and drew a deep breath, wringing her hands together to stop them from shaking. This feeling sorry for herself would get her nowhere.

After composing herself, Maggie leaned forward again and began fiddling with the radio knobs. This time she managed to find a station that was playing country and western songs. She turned it up and sat back in the seat.

Jack reached over and turned it down. "Were you trying to get a compliment from me?"

"No, and you didn't have to take me out last night and try to give me a good time just to make me feel better. I'll pay you back for everything you spent."

"I didn't do it just to make you feel better."

"Didn't you? Didn't you feel sorry for poor, stood-up Maggie? Let's make her feel good by giving her a night on the town? Don't get me wrong. I did enjoy it. I've never been to a French restaurant, and I wanted to go to a show, but you didn't need to do it out of charity." This time, tears oozed from her eyes and she was unable to keep them from sliding out from under her glasses.

He pounded his palm against the steering wheel. "Maggie, Maggie, that wasn't it."

"Yes, it was. I knew it. Even when I kissed you. I know you still love your wife... and I ... Well, it's not like I'm free anyway. That's why it was stupid to meet those men. Al may come back." Maggie stopped. She was rambling again. That sounded silly.

Fighting to bring her tears under control, she fumbled in her purse for a tissue. For a couple of minutes there was silence, as she tried to control her breathing. Finally she blew her nose. "I'm sorry, I didn't mean to get emotional."

"No, it's okay. I think we both let ourselves get carried away with the moment last night. I enjoyed it too. Even... even when you kissed me. But you don't need to get upset. It's not something that's going to be repeated."

He reached over and turned the radio back up, his movements quick and jerky. Maggie leaned back on the head rest and closed her eyes, letting the rhythm of the road and the soft sounds of the music lull her into sleep.

~ * ~

"How did the meeting go?" Billie asked, eyes wide and questioning, almost as soon as Maggie got in the door.

She didn't know what to say. Maggie had not expected that to be the first question on Billie's lips when she and Jack walked in the door, but she should have expected it. She'd been dodging the question every time they'd talked on the phone.

Billie didn't know about the latest jackpot win. Maggie wanted to tell the girls first. Still, Maggie would rather have waited to talk about the ill-fated date. Beside her, Jack put down her overstuffed suitcase and a new tote bag filled with the make-up she'd purchased. She wanted to tell him he didn't need to play bellhop. As it was, she feared he lingered because he wanted to hear what she told Billie. He'd made his feelings known on the drive home.

Maggie made a face, looking around the messy living room. Soda cans littered the coffee table alongside a pizza box and discarded paper plates that held congealed cheese and pieces of crust.

Billie seemed to notice the direction of Maggie's eyes. Her friend's face took on a pained look. "Oh, sorry. The girls had some friends over to watch a new video, and I stayed up late watching an all-night movie. I slept in this morning and didn't get a chance to clean up. I'll take care of it before I leave."

"Thanks, but I'll have a word with the girls. They know better than this."

"Well, I'll be going," Jack said, shifting from one leg to the next, almost as though waiting for an invitation to stay. Maggie wasn't about to issue one. Billie wasn't going to be put off much longer. She nodded shortly.

"Thanks for everything," she said, trying to keep the hard note out of her voice, but being unsuccessful. Even Billie raised her pencil-thin eyebrows.

Once the door was closed behind Jack, Maggie began picking up the pizza boxes and soda cans. Billie grabbed a wastebasket and joined her.

"So tell me," she said. "Before the girls come home. How was it?"

Maggie dumped a couple of plates into the wastebasket and then grabbed Billie's wrists, no longer able to keep her news to herself. She'd tell the girls when they got home, but she couldn't keep from telling Billie any longer. "Wait, put that down. Let me tell you something."

Billie's gray eyes narrowed as she put the wastebasket down. "What? Did someone do..." She stopped, taking hold of Maggie's trembling hand. "You're smiling."

Maggie squeezed Billie's hand tightly. "Billie, I played the milking game again. Quarters this time. Billie, I won ten thousand dollars!"

Billie's scream was like a banshee ringing through the little house. "Are you kidding?"

"No."

"Aaaahh!" Billie screamed again, throwing her arms around Maggie, and they began jumping up and down, hopping so hard and fast, the floors of the house groaned under their combined weight.

"Did they give you cash?" Billie asked as they calmed down. Tears poured from their eyes, Billie's black mascara carving dark lines on her cheek.

"A cashier's check," Maggie told her. She picked up her purse with shaking hands and took out the check, holding it up to Billie.

"Tell me all about it," Billie said, her hands as shaky Maggie's.

Maggie described the two old women who had suggested the quarter game and playing all the lines and then how she had played the game until the five cows all came up.

"Where was Jack?" Billie asked.

"Having breakfast. Wouldn't you know it? There I was, all alone in my moment of glory." She didn't want to think of Jack. Not after these crazy, confusing hours. She'd much rather think about the money.

"What are you going to do with it?" Billie asked.

"I haven't decided. I haven't even thought about it." Maggie glanced around the house. "Fix up the house maybe? Buy new furniture, clothes for the girls."

"Buy *you* some clothes," Billie said. "Do *your* hair. Hell, get a complete makeover. You need to do something for yourself for once, Maggie."

She wrinkled her nose. "That's kind of what this trip was all about and look what happened."

"What do you mean? The guy?" Billie grabbed her hand and pulled her to the sagging sofa. "Stop avoiding that and tell me about it. I want to know."

She might as well get it over with. Billie wasn't going to let the matter drop until she told her.

Maggie wrinkled her nose and shoved her glasses up her nose. "He was all right. Not my type."

"So what did you do?" Billie inquired.

"We had drinks. That was all. We both knew we weren't right for each other." That was a lie, but only through omission. They had known they were not right for each other. No need to tell Billie what a fool he had made of her. And there was no way she was telling Billie about Rich. The less said about that debacle, the better.

"Well, I hope you're over this crazy notion of meeting those guys from the computer."

"Billie, this was your idea. You and the girls were so sure I'd meet someone special on there. And Bob sounded nice online. He wanted to be my friend, to just talk. That man was ready to take me to his motel room five minutes after we met. How was I supposed to know he was a complete jerk in real life?"

Billie smiled sadly as Maggie again started to pick up the pizza boxes. Together they gathered them and the cans and straightened the living room. As Maggie surveyed the sofa with its stained, overstuffed arms and the threadbare carpet, she made a decision. They would get new furniture. She thought of Jack's house with its few pieces of nice furniture. Maybe he would be selling some of it when he left town.

"Did you know Jack was leaving in two months?" she asked Billie as they carried the trash into the kitchen. This room was just as big a disaster as the living room. The teens had left remnants of microwave popcorn--big greasy bowls and left over wrappers with a few black kernels inside. More soda cans and glasses with shriveled lemons were stacked on the counter. Billie issued another apology and began shoveling the wrappers into the wastebasket.

"Is Jack transferring?" she asked.

"Retiring," Maggie said. "Going home to New Mexico."

"Oh, now that I knew. Boy, you should have seen him when I told him where you were. He looked fit to be tied."

"Thanks for telling him," Maggie said unhappily. "He lectured me about fifty times about how I shouldn't be meeting people this way."

"Sorry. I should have known better. He's always been so protective of you."

"Protective?" Maggie asked. She stopped rinsing glasses in the sink and faced her friend.

"Yes, don't you think so? Whenever you need something, he's there."

Maggie rolled her eyes and resumed rinsing the glasses. "That's not protective. He just feels sorry for me."

"There's more to it than that."

"No, there isn't. And he has no right to be anything. He's just my neighbor. Okay, he's nice and he took me out to dinner last night and to a show, but…" Maggie stopped, as her cheeks grew hot.

Billie's face filled with open curiosity, her blue eyes large. "He took you out?"

"It wasn't a date," Maggie argued. "He was being nice. 'Cause he felt sorry for me. Poor old Maggie, charity case."

And that was still how she felt. She had felt rejected enough by that louse Bobcat. She hated to feel that way about Jack. Especially since he seemed to evoke these strange feelings inside her.

"I should set him up with someone before he leaves town," Billie said. "He is a nice guy."

"He's still in love with his wife," Maggie said shortly. "And it's awfully hard to compete against a ghost."

Billie stopped as she was about to light a cigarette. Her gaze grew shrewd. "Am I missing something here?"

"No," Maggie said quickly, filling the sink with hot water to wash the glasses and assorted silverware that was piled in the sink. "How are the girls doing? I didn't get a chance to talk with them this morning."

"They're fine, though I don't know when they'll be home. They decided to beat the heat and go to the movies after Sunday school."

"Nothing R-rated."

"No. Boy, do they enjoy that computer. I could barely get on there myself," Billie said with a laugh.

"They didn't fight over it, did they? They're constantly bickering over who spends more time on the darn thing."

"No, actually they were on it together."

"Together?" Maggie said in surprise.

Billie inhaled and then blew out a cloud of smoke. She tapped her long red nails on the counter as if she was considering something and then nodded shortly as though making a decision. "I might as well tell you 'cause you're going to find out anyway. April has been searching for Al."

"Al?" Maggie's heart skipped. "My Al?"

"Of course, your Al. But their Al, too."

Her heart was beginning to race. "Why would they do something like that? I know we talked about it once, but I told them that if he's coming back, he'll do it on his own. I don't want to chase him down. It's like I want something from him. I want him to come back so he can get to know the girls."

"And not for you?"

Maggie dropped her head. Until two months ago, she could have answered that easily. She wanted him to come back to get to know the girls and so that they could get to know him. Part of her even had some hazy thoughts about being with him again.

But the male attention on the computer and her close moments at dinner with Jack had shown her something she had not thought about until this moment. He had made her feel like a woman, a real woman with physical needs. The men on the computer had made her feel like a special woman. And that was what she wanted. Maggie wanted to share her life with a man, but not just any man. She wanted Al, but mostly, she wanted love.

~ * ~

Jack waited until Billie was gone. He knew the two would want to chatter on about the jackpot win and about the date that never was. He'd almost wanted to hear Maggie's take on it as she presented it to Billie but he doubted she would have said anything in front of him.

He paced his house as he waited, replaying the scene in the car and her tears over and over. He'd handled that so badly. But he hadn't come in contact with a woman's emotions in a long time.

Not that he'd ever been good with emotional scenes. Carla had been used to that side of him, though he had always tried to be particularly sensitive to her needs.

Minutes after Billie drove away from the house, Jack crossed the front lawn and knocked on Maggie's door. The midday heat pressed down on him, but he wanted to do this before the twins came home.

Maggie had changed into a t-shirt and baggy shorts, and he noted she had washed off the make-up she had been wearing earlier. That was fine. He thought she looked better without it. He wasn't going to tell her that. She seemed to have developed a thin skin where he was concerned.

Her eyes were wide with surprise when she saw him, but she ushered him inside. The air conditioner labored, and it was still only May.

"I may get a new air conditioner with my winnings," she said, brushing her hair behind one ear. "Would you like some lemonade? I was just about to make up a batch."

"Sure. That would be fine."

He was pleased she was being civil after they had both been so quiet on the drive home following their emotional argument. Maybe she felt as badly about it as he did. He followed her into the kitchen and sat at the table to watch as she began cutting up lemons.

"I wanted to apologize," he began.

"No need." Maggie kept her face averted, her gaze directed at the lemons as though they were the most fascinating objects in the world.

"Yes, there is. I wasn't being charitable with you last night. I enjoyed the evening."

"So did I," she said in a quiet voice.

"Look, I'm only going to be here for two more months," he added, realizing his throat was very dry. "I think we should go out again." He swallowed, the sound audible in the quiet room.

Maggie's jaw dropped and then she clamped her mouth shut. He had surprised her.

"Like a date?" she questioned, her eyes blinking very rapidly behind the thick lenses of her glasses.

Jack sighed heavily. He didn't know what to call it. He just wanted to spend time with her, social time, not time when they were cleaning the yard or fixing her car or painting the fence. He wanted to see more smiles such as she had given him over dinner. He wanted to feel that alive-sensation he'd had as he watched her enthusiasm over the show.

He could see her expectant gaze, but he avoided her question about a date. That might turn them both awkward again.

"The base is having its annual picnic in a couple of weeks. I thought maybe you and the girls might like to go."

Her eyes grew wide and her face lit up slowly until she was beaming. It was like she had won another ten thousand dollars, and her smile sent a surge of electricity racing through him. He was probably making a mistake, he told himself. But after all, he was only going to be there for two more months.

Ten

"Do you want me to be a beauty? Change my looks so you'll love me more?" the woman intoned in a song that blared from the car radio. It might have been written for Maggie. "Is that the way to win your love? I'll try 'cause you're more man than I've known before."

Maggie sighed heavily as she turned the car onto the main street in downtown Cactus Bluffs, her mind still on the song. Women changed so much to please men. Like Billie. Normally her friend wore her red hair tied in a pony tail, and her work clothes consisted of jeans and cotton tops like Maggie. On Saturday nights, her friend transformed into a different person. She went dancing at local bars, wearing short skirts and flashy jewelry. Her red hair would be curled and her make-up was so thick men who saw her later at the store barely recognized her.

Billie urged Maggie to try the same thing, but she resisted. Why had she never done that? The answer was simple. Maggie had never wanted to change or meet someone knew because she was sure Al would come back.

Why dress up now? Because Jack invited her to a picnic? Because she wanted Jack to look at her as more than just the pudgy neighbor lady with the noisy kids and roaming dog?

"Maggie, give it up," she whispered to herself. Jack wasn't going to look at her just because she changed her looks. He knew the real Maggie.

Yet, what was wrong with looking better? The computer proved Maggie could attract men. They wanted to meet her based on her wit. Could she attract anyone if she made changes in her looks? She doubted it.

Maggie turned off the radio. It depressed her. Her eyes scanned the wide street for a parking spot. Downtown Cactus Bluffs was normally empty at midday in the middle of the week, but parking was always at a premium. Most of the parking along the main street had been eliminated to make room for another lane of traffic. That way cars could pass at will as they drove through town. The crush of traffic happened only on Fridays and sometimes just before a holiday weekend. In the meantime, downtown parking had been pushed to the rear of the business district or to a lot at one end of the three-block main street.

One of the businesses that fronted on the main street was Zamora's Opticians. Maggie normally stopped there every year to check her eyes. Today she was stopping in because she was getting contacts. The initial inquiries had been made after the first jackpot win. Now she was going through with the idea. Today they would arrive.

The new eyewear was only the beginning. After this stop she would pick up the girls from school, and they would travel to a mall located in a Los Angeles suburb. The plan was to get new summer clothes for the girls, but Maggie needed some things for herself as well.

It wasn't because she wanted to change. She already had. This morning her bathroom scale showed that she'd lost more than twenty pounds in the past two months. Her jeans no longer fit without a belt. They literally bagged on her hips and thighs. Her hips, which had once protruded with wide prominence, had rounded into gentle curves, her thighs growing sculpted and rounded.

More than the computer had done the job. Besides changing her eating habits to be online, Maggie had started an exercise program.

The town had one co-ed gym, and her jackpot money paid the bill for joining. She was working a dayside shift at the moment, so every morning after Jack and the girls left, Maggie went to the gym for an hour and got on the treadmill.

Jack was responsible for the idea, but not because she wanted to look good for him. While she'd been cleaning his house when he was away, Maggie discovered that his second bedroom contained a home gym. She'd been tempted to try the rowing machine, but feared she might mess up the settings. It explained how he kept in such great physical shape.

The exercise had Maggie feeling better about herself. Suddenly she no longer viewed herself as "plain old Maggie." The men on the computer had showed her that she could be witty. Now her daily workouts were demonstrating she could be fit as well. Thin was not necessarily her goal or even within her realm of thinking. She wasn't built that way. And she would never want anyone whose emphasis was on looks--men like Rich or Bob.

The idea of meeting men on the computer was a thing of the past. She had not done much chatting since coming home from Las Vegas. While she had enjoyed the attention, she had also learned a big lesson about honesty--both on her part and theirs as well.

An open parking space loomed ahead, and Maggie whipped her car into it. It was two doors down from the eye doctor's office. As Maggie removed her glasses for the doctor, she drew a deep breath. This was like starting a new life.

~ * ~

Maggie sat back in the chair, trying not to look at the mirror and the strange aluminum strips that stuck out from her head. With the plastic wrapped around her shoulders, and her hair protruding from the strips at odd angles, Maggie resembled something out of a space movie.

The things women did for beauty. She looked down at her freshly manicured nails with the dark rose color. They were almost an inch longer than normal--products of an acrylic wrap.

In another fifteen minutes or so, her hair would be different too. Was she being silly? Maggie had never done such a drastic make over before. Her hair had been the same since high school.

What would the girls think? Maggie had not told them what she intended to do. The two were shopping and would return in half an hour. Would they be shocked or tease her? They were already gently ribbing Maggie about buying new clothes, though she could tell they were happy to see her taking an interest in her appearance. If they guessed why, they never let on. She told herself she wasn't doing this for Jack. The changes were for herself, and they'd started when she'd won her first jackpot.

Maggie blinked her eyes open as the stylist took hold of her shoulder. She'd fallen asleep. Reaching for her glasses, she realized they were gone. The new contacts felt strange in her eyes, but she liked being without the thick glasses she'd worn since she was eight. Her face looked different, and she could actually see. The twins were excited about them. Wait until they saw her hair. The stylist took her to a sink and began removing the strips.

"Mom, what are you doing?" April's shriek was a surprise. The girls had returned and stood by her holding several packages.

"I'm having my hair lightened," she said. The stylist continued her work as though the girls weren't leaning over her.

"Going bleached blonde?" May asked critically.

"No, just lighter. How was the shopping?"

They held up their bags. "I still have a couple more stops to make," April said. "May rushed me."

"You might as well go back," Maggie offered.

April stuck her tongue out at May. "See? I told you she wouldn't be ready."

The stylist had finished removing the strips and began rinsing her hair. She wrapped it in a towel when she was finished, and Maggie walked back to the chair with the girls. Maggie stared at her hair as the towel came off. The strange light color was a shock, but at the same time it was very pleasing. Its golden color made her face seem pinker and took away some of the pastiness. Beside her, the girls surprised faces reflected in the mirror.

"Wow, Mom, that color is great. Jack's going to think you're a blonde bombshell," April said, gently touching a damp curl.

"I'm not doing this for Jack," Maggie protested, turning her head from one side to the next. Despite her words, she couldn't help but wonder what he would think of her new look.

~ * ~

The noise of the gathering came to them through the opened car windows as they arrived. Shouts and laughter bubbled from the colorful throng that swarmed across the shores of Lake Hancock. A few heads bobbed in the water of the lake while others gamboled near the shoreline.

Lake Hancock was a stretch of azure in a sea of beige some 20 miles from Cactus Bluffs. No one knew why the lake had formed where there should be nothing but sand, rocks and cactus. The damp acreage had fostered the growth of a grove of cottonwood trees along one edge and that had been turned into a park.

A large brick barbeque pit squatted beside a shelter that hovered over long rows of picnic tables. This was where the Base held its annual picnic. It was always held in May, before the torrid heat of summer made outdoor eating in the midday impossible.

As Jack parked the car, April and May were already tugging at Maggie's shoulder from the back seat.

"May we go swimming?" April asked. "We'll find you."

"Yes, go on," she said with a laugh. All the girls could talk about all week was going swimming in the lake, though Maggie suspected they really wanted to show off the new suits purchased during their shopping adventure.

"You should put on sun block first." The warning came from Jack, and Maggie smiled her thanks at him. She'd nearly forgotten. He was watching both girls with a smile of patient indulgence.

May produced a tube from her bag and began slathering it over her bare arms. April was pulling off her shorts to reveal her suit underneath. After a frenzy of activity, they leaped from the car and started running across the rocky terrain. At least they attempted to run. Their sandals turned it more into an awkward race walk.

Maggie watched their departure and breathed a quick sigh of relief, though she felt their absence almost immediately. She and Jack were alone and the inside of the SUV seemed empty and hollow.

She had known she was going to be alone with Jack for part of the day. The girls had friends at the picnic and would be off socializing with them. Billie would not be around, but luckily, she did know some of the women who would be at the picnic.

Being with Jack was exciting and a little daunting, though in the past two weeks since her return from Las Vegas, Maggie forced herself back into the thought that he was just her neighbor. Her pulse still acted up when he stood close to her, and an accidental brush of his arm against hers could send tingles along her skin, but she kept reminding herself there would never be anything between them.

He'd come over a few evenings and cooked with the girls while Maggie worked. The girls had never shown an affinity for cooking before, but under Jack's guidance they were now becoming proficient at everything from baby back ribs to lasagna to enchiladas. Even fresh strawberry pie had been on the menu one night.

Maggie blinked her eyes rapidly. She was still having trouble dealing with the new contacts. Her eyes constantly felt dry or like they were being scratched. Jack had only stared at her in amazement when he saw her without her glasses.

After getting her bag out of the SUV, she turned to find Jack standing at the front bumper, watching her.

"You look very nice today," he said. "New clothes, new look."

Maggie's face grew warm with pleasure. She had taken time to put on make up this morning. During their shopping expedition, after getting her hair done, she had let the girls talk her into having a make over at the cosmetics' counter in one of the department stores. She'd spent more than she wanted of her jackpot money, but the result was much more natural than the garish make-up she'd applied when she went to Las Vegas.

She touched her new denim culottes, patting her hip as she always did. "I needed to get some new things. I've lost weight…"

"And you're looking very good," he said with an approving nod of his dark head and a quick wink.

The compliment sent a glow of pleasure bubbling through her insides. Maggie could only murmur a quick thanks.

"I can't get over how different you look without your glasses. I never knew you had such pretty eyes."

She blinked again, unused to such compliments, though they were elevating her pulse level. "Must be the contacts," she said with a shrug. "Though it's going to take me forever to get used to them."

He touched the tip of her nose. "Now I can see your freckles."

His touch was electric. She jerked her hand to her face and their fingers brushed. More electricity surged through her, a current that sizzled up her arm.

"That's not a compliment," she said, running her finger up and down her nose. "I've tried to hide those for years. Even that expensive make-up won't do it."

"You're not making all these changes because of those online boyfriends, are you? Don't tell me you're thinking of going off to meet another one?"

Maggie jerked her shocked gaze to his, feeling as though she'd been struck. She started to shake her head, and then realized he was smiling. His blue eyes danced with merriment; he was teasing.

"No. I'm through with that foolishness. Though maybe they are partially responsible for this."

"And I thought it was me," he said, black eyebrows arching.

She blinked, and this time it had nothing to do with the contacts. His blue eyes continued to dance with mischief, and she felt the crazy dancing in her stomach that he seemed to evoke so easily.

Maggie again told herself she wasn't changing because of Jack. No, the more she thought about it, the more she realized she wanted to do this for herself. The jackpot wins had her feeling like a winner; she wanted to look like one. Never again would anyone make her feel like a loser, as Bobcat and Ricardo had. Their looks of rejection still stung.

She turned aside those unpleasant thoughts and turned back to Jack. She slapped at his arm in a show of playfulness. "Stop teasing me, Jack."

He stopped, standing so close to her that she could smell the subtle scent of his cologne. He looked wonderful today in a dark polo shirt and khaki Bermuda shorts. His tanned face brought out the cobalt color of his eyes, and she noticed the thick black lashes that fringed them. What would it be like to touch his face, to trace her fingers along the chiseled edges of his firm jaw, to feel the smooth skin of his cheeks, or perhaps run her fingers over their roughness in the morning before he shaved?

A shiver of awareness and anticipation raced through her and Maggie turned away began walking toward the picnic area, forcing her quickened breath to slow down. As they approached the main area, she was aware of glances in their direction, even some stares. A few of the men waved at Jack.

She was pleased when Virginia Garcia waved them over. The plump, pleasant woman was a regular visitor to the store. She was married to an officer at the base, and her daughter was in the same class as April and May.

"Maggie, I haven't seen you since the spring pageant," she said, holding out her hands and then hugging Maggie. "You're looking gorgeous. What have you done to yourself?"

Maggie's cheeks grew warm and she smiled appreciatively, brushing at her hair. The wayward curl was gone for once, cut to a short length to blend in with the rest of her shortened hair. "Not much."

Virginia moved closer to her. "New do, and no glasses, and I swear you've lost weight. Wow." She turned to Jack, put out her hand and introduced herself.

Maggie winced at her omission. She should have remembered to introduce them. Virginia's husband, Captain Dick Garcia, approached. He nodded at Maggie and turned to Jack. They already knew each other and shook hands.

"Tell me about this winning streak of yours," Virginia said, tapping Maggie on the arm. "Listen to this, Dick. She's done what we're always hoping to do."

Maggie explained her jackpot wins. She could feel Jack's eyes on her as she talked. Several times she had to clasp her hands together, since she felt like they were flaying about wildly. Sometimes her hands became too animated when she got excited while talking. As her story concluded, she realized several other people had joined the group and were listening. Normally being the center of such attention frightened her, but the sight of Jack's amused grin calmed her nerves, even as it lit little fires in the pit of her stomach.

"You're a real winner," Virginia said, patting Maggie on the shoulder.

"That's what I keep telling her," Jack said. He put his hand on her other shoulder, and it singed her skin through the thin cotton. She smiled at him, worrying that she had taken too much attention with her story.

As the group began to trade their Las Vegas stories, she turned to him. "Am I talking too much?" she asked in a low voice.

"You don't talk enough," he said with a wink.

"Jack doesn't even go to Vegas," one of the younger men said.

Jack leaned toward Maggie. "She's gotten me there a couple of times." His wink sent a thrill through her, but this time there was more to it.

Suddenly everything seemed to explode around her. Maggie couldn't remember the last time she had experienced such joy, such pleasure with everything. She'd been to picnics before, but always as the girls' mother. Today she was part of a couple, or at least people saw it that way, even if she and Jack only considered it a friendly outing. No matter how it might be labeled, she was with someone, and it felt wonderful.

As Virginia and some of the other women decided it was time to start preparing the food, she volunteered.

"You can help us prepare the salads," Virginia said, taking Maggie's arm. She leaned close to Maggie as they walked away, casting a quick glance back at Jack. "That guy is a hunk! How come you've never brought him to any of the school events?"

"He's my neighbor," Maggie explained, looking toward him. "And I saw the look in your eye. We're just friends."

"Nothing wrong with hoping."

"Exactly," Nancy Allen said from the other side of Virginia. "I've known Jack Conroy since he got here, and he never goes out. I've always said he needs to socialize more."

"Maybe," Maggie said, but the thought of him taking someone else out suddenly bothered her. She found herself looking back at him as they arrived at the line of food tables. What would it be like to be with Jack as more than a friend? She thought of their evening together in Las Vegas. He had been a very considerate man, and it would have been nice to have been his date.

"Do you know how his wife died?" Maggie asked Nancy as they began taking plastic wrap off the tops of large salad bowls. "I've always been afraid to ask."

"Car accident," Nancy replied grimly. "I don't think he talks about it. I just heard it through the grapevine. He's been over to the house for parties, but he always comes alone, and I think most of the time, he comes just to be polite. He never stays long."

Maggie knew what she meant. He'd always been very polite, but she'd never seen him go out of the way to be social.

"I think that's why he invited me. Out of politeness because he knew the girls wanted to come," Maggie said.

Nancy and Virginia traded knowing looks.

"What?" Maggie asked, looking from one to the other.

Virginia shook her head, dark hair dancing around her plump, olive face. "I don't think he's looking at you like the polite, next-door neighbor."

"No," Nancy agreed. "I think he has more on his mind than being polite. Mark my words."

Both women laughed, and Maggie felt her cheeks burn. At the same time, a small ray of hope grew in her head. Was that possible? Could Jack see her as more than his neighbor?

~ * ~

Jack savored the sight of Maggie at the picnic. He'd always liked watching her tell stories, either to the girls or in the store to Billie. She did much of the explaining with quick waves of her expressive hands.

Her eyes danced as she told the assembled group about winning the jackpot.

Her eyes--now they were something else. Seeing her without her glasses had surprised him, but what shocked him more was how she looked without them. He'd always thought their thickness made her eyes look bigger. Maybe they had, but they'd also concealed the golden lights that glowed in her eyes and sparkled to life as she became animated and excited.

He couldn't get over the changes in her. Everything about her seemed different today--from the top of her newly golden hair that glimmered in the sun to the tips of her rose-colored toenails. The denim culottes she wore showed the rounded curves of her hips while also displaying a narrow waistline.

When had the changes come? He'd been with her and her girls almost every day for the past two weeks, and he was enjoying being around them. He couldn't remember the last time he'd looked forward to finishing work just to get home and see what they might do that evening.

At the same time, he was beginning to have a problem. The more he was around Maggie, the more he wanted to be near her. It was as though she was becoming addictive. What would he do in six weeks when it was time to leave?

She walked toward him, her movements slow and graceful. She'd always been graceful, even when she was heavier, though he doubted she realized it, given her constant belittling of herself. Today she was receiving compliments, and he was pleased people were taking note of her. So often people came into the store, and she might as well have been one of the fixtures. Maggie had always been special. He'd known it; he was pleased others were noticing it as well.

"Should we get a table?" she asked as she looked around them. Some of the families were starting to lay claims to picnic tables.

"Anyone in particular you want to sit with?" he asked. He wanted her to feel comfortable.

"Virginia asked if we wanted to sit with them. The girls are with her daughter, Kit."

"Then let's go sit with them. I don't know Dick, but I've seen him around, and he seems like a top notch guy."

He was willing to do just about anything to see her smile. She'd been very matter-of-fact with him since they had returned from Las Vegas. He was trying hard to let her know that he spent time with her because he enjoyed her company, not because he felt sorry for her. Hopefully his actions spoke for themselves. Actually, he looked forward to cooking with the girls and watching Maggie's expressions as she tasted their concoctions.

Together, they gathered up plates and supplies and took them over to join the Garcia family. The girls were still in the water playing a spirited game of water polo with the others, though it was starting to break up.

Maggie and Virginia called them out and after drying the girls off, they got into the line for hotdogs, hamburgers and all the fixings.

Lunch was a lively affair, though Jack and Maggie didn't say much. The girls did most of the talking, and as he often did, Jack found himself watching Maggie. As always, he could see the pride that shone in her eyes when her girls spoke.

When lunch ended, the girls took a walk and he relaxed at the base of a tree while Maggie helped the women clean up. Finally she came over to him. Jack had been half dozing in the heat of the early afternoon.

"You're being antisocial," she told him, sitting on a patch of blanket next to him.

He shrugged. "I just felt like relaxing."

"You felt like sleeping," she teased, brown eyes coming alive. "Don't think I didn't notice you had your eyes closed for a while there."

"I was pretending."

"Right," she said with a giggle. She shifted, turning to glance to where the girls were walking at the edge of the lake. "Thanks for bringing us, Jack. The girls are having a great time. They've always wanted to come to a base function. So many of their friends go. It will be the talk of school on Monday."

"Well, I did it for you, too," he said.

"Me?" Her cheeks colored slightly, eyes wide as she looked at him.

He wanted to touch her. To reach out and brush his fingers over the soft skin of her bare upper arms. Maybe seek out the pulse in her fair neck. "You deserve to have people do good things for you, Maggie."

The color rose to a very pleasant shade of pink. "No." Then she laughed. "Don't say I'm a winner again, just because I won that jackpot. Everyone keeps saying that."

"You are a winner and not just because of the winning."

Her shoulders rolled in a shrug and her eyes dropped as though she was embarrassed. "So now what? Are you going to join that volleyball game?"

Jack grimaced. He didn't want to make her feel uncomfortable. "I'm terrible at team sports. I was thinking of going swimming. What do you say, shall we take a dip to cool off?"

She blinked rapidly and drew back. "Swimming? Me? The whale? In a suit?"

"You're not a whale," he corrected.

She patted her hips. "Oh, I know. I've lost some weight, but I still don't have the nerve to let people see my bare body."

"There's nothing wrong with your body," he said. "I think it's very nicely..." he stopped, feeling warm under the collar.

"Nicely what?" she asked, leaning toward him, lifting and lowering her eyebrows as Billie often did when teasing in a sexual manner. "You can't just say that without explaining more."

Jack's breath caught. Was she flirting with him? The thought turned him warm inside. His eyes dropped from her face to the curve of her breasts, to the nipped in waist to the flaring hips and nice length of her legs. "Okay, you've become very nicely curved," he said through very dry lips.

Again the color rose in her cheeks and he was tempted to touch their softness. She pushed herself to her feet. "I'd rather go for a walk."

Jack held out his hand and she looked at it for a second as though uncertain what to do with it. She took hold of it finally and pulled him up. The touch was gentle but it was like piercing him with a red hot poker. His eyes met hers and he realized her breath was coming a little faster. Her chest heaved once, and he had to let her hand go, or he might have been in trouble.

As they walked away from the picnic area, he led her up a wash, shaded by scrub brush. It was dry now, its center eaten away by time and flash floods. The going was rocky, and he found he had to help her up the rocks several times. They reached the top of the short canyon and shielded from the sun by a large boulder, they looked down toward the picnic area.

She waved down toward the girls who were back in the water, though at the edge. "Do you suppose they can see us?" she asked.

"If they're looking," he said, studying her. He reached up and put his finger on her nose. "You know you were so careful with the girls, making certain they were covered with suntan oil and you're beginning to burn."

She touched her nose. "Oh, my gosh."

"Gives you more freckles too," he teased.

She gazed up at him, eyes wide and uncertain. Jack felt like he was being hypnotized by the gold flecks in her eyes. She licked her lips and he moved his gaze down, finding himself fascinated with her very pink--and now moist--lips. He thought about her spontaneous kiss at the casino when she won and how it had melted him inside. He wanted to feel that way again.

Before he could convince himself he was being foolish, Jack reacted. Catching her chin in his hand, he leaned toward her. Maggie's breath touched his cheek, quick and uneven, but she stayed still, lifting her eyes to meet his. For few long seconds their eyes held, as though there was an invisible link between them. Her hands rested against his chest and he could feel their warmth even through the material of his shirt.

All his senses were on alert, and his body grew heated with red hot desire. He leaned toward her, testing the warm lips gently. She moaned under his touch, and he deepened the kiss, tasting her sweetness. His blood grew hot as molten lava and every masculine inch of him throbbed to life.

He wanted the moment never to end. His hands caught her arms and pulled her close to him. Her warm body pressed itself to his. Her curves were delightful against him and his hands moved over her back, exploring the curve of her waist and hip as his tongue inched between her lips, exploring the warm moistness of her mouth.

She whimpered deep in her throat and his hand moved up to touch her soft breast.

The touch was electric, and her hand caught his before he could fully explore the wonderful curve. She suddenly jerked away, blinking.

Maggie stared at him with suddenly frightened eyes, confusion filling their fiery depths. He could see the soft flames of desire in her eyes, but they were filled with shock and fear as well.

Her breath came in shallow gasps and she shook her head. Jack drew back, cursing himself for giving in to his urges. He dropped his head, took a deep breath and turned away.

"I'm sorry," he said.

"No, I am," she said, dropping her head. "I'm not real good at this. I'm... you know... there hasn't been anyone in my life since Al..." She shoved her hair out of her face, her breath coming quickly and Jack stepped back from her.

He knew what she was saying. And he knew how hopeless this situation was. Maggie had never given herself to a man since Al, and he doubted she would ever want to be with anyone else.

"I'm sorry," he said again. "I guess we both just got caught up in the heat of the moment."

She nodded saying nothing.

"We better go back," he said.

The trip down hill went much quicker than their trip up. While he had helped Maggie over rocks as they climbed, this time she stayed far enough away from him that she could do everything on her own.

He wanted to tell her it was okay. He wasn't going to try to kiss her again, but as they reached the bottom and he watched her walk away, he felt very sad. He had no idea what would happen now.

Eleven

The trip back to town was silent. The twins had worn themselves out in the water and playing under the hot sun. They both fell soundly asleep.

Maggie was tired from too much sun also. She kept finding herself glancing across the seat at Jack. Thank goodness for the need for dark glasses.

Jack had kissed her! Really kissed her! It had nothing to do with making her feel good. Whatever he had done, he had done it by choice. It was a moment Maggie doubted she would ever forget.

As their eyes had met, his bright blue eyes had grown warm with desire. Maggie had felt seventeen again, sitting in the backseat close to Al Williams. Her stomach had been a mass of butterflies and a strange warmth had flooded her lower regions. Her breath had caught as he'd lowered his face to her. His lips had been soft, against hers, intoxicating. She had savored the touch, wanting more, and almost too quickly, it had been over.

Now she found she couldn't stop looking at him. Jack Conroy. Suddenly he was no longer just the handsome man next door. For four years he'd lived there, and she'd never wanted to get to know him better. Now he would be gone in less than two months, and she wanted to know everything about him.

Maggie had no idea how to get to know him. Invite him for dinner? Ask him to share his thoughts, his feelings for his dead wife? Since Al Williams, she'd never dated, never had any idea how to capture a man. Flirting online had seemed like a possible answer, but that hadn't worked. It might be fun, but it wouldn't replace a flesh and blood man. Until today, until that kiss, she'd never thought she needed a real man. Damn! Why couldn't Al come back?

Jack turned toward Maggie as though he knew what she was thinking. "Did you enjoy the picnic?"

"Yes," she said with a vigorous nod. "Thanks for inviting us."

He nodded sharply. "I'm pleased. I should invite the girls to more events on the base before I leave. That way, they will have friends who might invite them later."

"They'd love that, although they already know the Garcias and Colonel McCoy's girls. Are you going to his birthday party next week?"

The Colonel's wife had extended an invitation to Maggie as they'd cleaned up the tables, but she had a feeling it was meant if she went with Jack.

He frowned. "I hadn't thought about it, but I suppose I should. Would you like to go with me?"

Her breath caught. Did he really mean that? He would take her? "I... well, I..."

"You don't have to go if you don't want," he said, turning his attention back to the road.

"No, I'd love to go," Maggie said, fearing she was speaking too loudly and too quickly. "It's just..."

"What?"

She thought about Virginia's comments and about appearances.

"What's the problem?" he repeated.

Licking her dry lips, Maggie tried to figure out how to phrase what she needed to say.

"It might seem like a date," she concluded finally.

Jack's smile was quick and pleasant. "Good. Let it be a date."

Her breath caught again. "Really? A date?" She pressed her lips together, fighting a smile and wishing she hadn't sounded so incredulous.

He nodded slowly as he glanced over at her again. "I've made a decision, Maggie. You need to get out more. There were two or three men from that picnic today who might want to give you a call. Or ask you to the Colonel's party. If you'd rather go with them, it's all right. I'll understand."

Maggie couldn't imagine wanting to go with anyone but Jack, but then the rest of his words registered. He wanted her to get out more. "Why would you do that?"

"Because before I leave town, I'm going to turn you into the princess of Cactus Bluffs. You're a late bloomer, Maggie Hemple, but like a desert rose, you're finally beginning to blossom."

Her cheeks burned, and Maggie knew she wore a healthy blush. "Did you get a sunburn, or are you blushing?" he teased.

"Both," she replied. His compliments were wonderful and had her beaming like a school girl. At the same time, she didn't really like what he was saying. He wanted to make her seem like a prize, but not for himself, for someone else.

~ * ~

"I think Jack likes you," April said as they walked inside after Jack dropped them off at the house. The interior was hot after the coolness of the air-conditioned car. Both girls flung themselves onto the sofa.

"Don't even start that," Maggie said, going over to the air conditioner and flipping it on to high. She would keep it there until the house cooled off. She glanced toward the girls, who were watching her, and shook her head. "You're seeing things. And remember, he's leaving in a couple of months."

"Too bad we can't go with him and get out of this dump," May grumbled, pounding her hand on the beat up sofa.

Maggie looked from one to the other. This opened another door, one that had been beckoning her lately. Perhaps it was why she had not spent more of the jackpot winnings. She walked over to the chair that faced the sofa and sat down. "Do you want to get away from here? What about Granddad and Grandma? Your cousins?"

"We have cousins in Los Angeles," April said. "We see them, so it's not like they would be lost forever."

That had been Maggie's thinking, but she did not want to go if it meant making the girls unhappy. "Well," she said, drawing a deep breath, "what if we took the rest of that jackpot money and used it to leave? Would you like that? I guess I could get a new job just about anywhere."

April shrugged a thin shoulder. Her blue eyes looked troubled as they met Maggie's. "To be honest? After Jack leaves, I don't care."

May's eyes were solemn as she nodded in agreement. "I love Grandma, but we could still come to see her. Our friends come and go as their parents get transferred. Kit Garcia says her Dad will have to move next winter, so they'll be gone."

Maggie drew a deep breath. Maybe the time had come to start thinking about going. Moving. The idea was frightening, but at the same time, for once, she realized she could do it. As long as she had the girls, she could handle just about anything.

She caught her reflection in the mirror across the room. Her nose was red and sunburned, but for once, in her eyes she saw something else. Confidence. Where had it come from? Winning those jackpots? Going out on her own and surviving those two awful men who snubbed her?

No, a lot had to do with Jack. Being around him, being with him had made her feel more womanly than she'd ever felt. Maggie's eyes flickered out the window to where Jack was setting out his sprinklers to water the lawn. Her fingers brushed her lips, recalling his kiss. She hated the thought of his not being around. If he wasn't leaving, she doubted she would want to leave Cactus Bluffs, but the town would not be the same once he was gone. And this time she wasn't going to wait around.

~ * ~

He'd compared her to a desert flower, but that wasn't what Jack felt as Maggie opened the door to him on their way to the Colonel's party. All he could do was stare at her.

Maggie had tied her hair on top of her head again, and put on make-up, just a light touch though, outlining her brown eyes that were big and glowing without the glasses. Her sun dress was a pale yellow that stood out against her tanned chest, its low front showing the full lines of her breasts and nipping in to show her receding waist. The skirt flared out about her curvy hips. Her full lips were outlined in a delicate pink, much better than the heavy red she had worn in Las Vegas.

This wasn't a date, he reminded himself. He was doing this to get Maggie into the social whirl more. Maybe before he left, she might meet someone she liked, and it was showing all the men at the base that there was more to Maggie Hemple than just the pleasant woman who took their change for soda and gas.

Thoughts of Carla invaded, but only momentarily. Lately he'd been finding himself comparing the two, but they were too different. He couldn't imagine Carla chasing through the mud after a dog as he saw Maggie do, but the sight made him smile. He couldn't imagine Carla being as self-sacrificing as Maggie was with her twins. Carla always thought of herself first. No, that wasn't fair. She thought of herself after Jack. He forced away thoughts of Carla as he turned to Maggie.

"You look beautiful," he said, his blood growing warm at the sight of her blushing cheeks. Even that reaction was endearing. Carla had always taken her looks for granted.

"Thanks, and you, sir, are quite the handsome lad." Maggie's delightful laugh filled the room.

Billie looked up from her seat at the computer. She was staying with the twins for the evening. "Hey, you do look good, Conroy. If I'd known you could clean up that well, I'd have gone after you a long time ago myself."

He winked at her. "And if I thought I could compete with those online guys of yours, I might have gone after you."

She waved at the computer. "It's a fantasy world." Her eyes fell to Maggie. "As you found out, right?"

Maggie's face turned a healthy shade of pink. "Yes, mother hen. I'm going to say good night to the girls. I'll be ready in a second." She disappeared into the hall.

Jack turned to Billie who had been watching him, her eyes shrewd.

"She's something else," Billie said, "but you know that, don't you?"

Jack shoved his hands in his pockets, shifting from one foot to the next. He tried to turn the question back on her. "What do you mean?"

She tapped an unlit cigarette on the desk top, but made no attempt to light it. "I've seen the way you look at her when you come into the store. Or just now, for that matter. If I were her father, I'd be asking your intentions, young man."

He inhaled sharply, shaking his head. "I'm leaving next month."

"Just like that. You and Al. You guys come and go."

Jack started to protest, but Billie held up a thin hand.

"You're no Al Williams, and that might be worse."

Her words surprised him and stared down at her. "Why?"

"Because like I said, I've seen how you look at her. Can you stand to go and leave her here?"

The words were like a blow delivered to his midsection. Jack turned away as a pain shook his insides. "I have to," he said quietly. "There's nothing I can offer her. She's waiting for Al."

"And looking at you," Billie said bluntly. "Wanting you. Can't you see that? She's changed."

"Not because of me." he protested. "I want her to get out, to meet other guys."

"And if she does?" Billie asked. She looked at the cigarette as though realizing it was in her hand and tossed it aside. A laugh rang out, sudden and unexpected as she shook her head. "You're both fooling yourselves. Why haven't you remarried, Jack? And be honest. No one can replace your wife, or you don't want to hurt again? Which? I've heard it all."

He didn't want to get into this discussion with Billie, so he simply shook his head. He wanted to call down the hall for Maggie, but he feared she would walk into the middle of the discussion.

Billie's voice was relentless. "It's too late to stop the hurt, Jack. It's going to hurt like hell to leave her and those girls. And if your wife was so wonderful, then she would want you to be happy. Don't forget her, just move on with your life."

Maggie's footsteps clicked in the hall. He nodded at Billie, eager to get away from her and walked toward the front door.

~ * ~

The armory had been festooned with balloons for the Colonel's birthday party. Maggie found herself glancing at Jack from time to time, excited about being with him. She had thought of little but him since the picnic. She'd lost more weight because her appetite had disappeared while her hours at the gym had expanded. Sitting on the exercise bike provided a good opportunity to daydream about Jack.

It had been a long time since she'd felt so good. With that had come the certainty that she didn't want him to see her as just Maggie. She wanted him to see more than a blooming flower.

As they entered the dance, Maggie waved at several people she had met at the picnic. Tables had been arranged around the large wooden floor, and in one corner, a country western band strummed out a tune about heartbreak. Crepe paper banners dripped from low wires strung well below the vaulted ceiling. Some of the women were putting out food and Maggie excused herself to join them.

"Hi, Maggie," Virginia said, welcoming her over. "I'm so glad you and Jack decided to come."

You and Jack. It sounded like they were a couple. Maggie nodded happily. There was something exciting about being with Jack, about being considered his date. Six months ago, she could never have imagined it.

"You can put your sweater and bag over at that table," Lydia Grange told her. "We've already saved it."

Maggie was surprised to feel so at home, like part of the group. So many years she had spent in Cactus Bluffs, and she had waited on almost all these women at one time or another. She had always known them, but had never dreamed of socializing with them, or having one of them invite her to sit at their table. It had to be Jack. Or her new looks? Would any of them have been friends with the old Maggie Hemple?

No, they might have been friendly to her. The old Maggie would not have considered herself good enough to be friends with them. Forcing aside those thoughts, she busied herself helping them set out plates for cake and replenish the punch. As some drifted away to dance, she found Jack standing beside her.

"Shall we try this?" He motioned toward the dance floor.

The thought of being in his arms was heavenly and Maggie let him walk her toward the floor. At least this time she wasn't as stiff as Las Vegas. She would never admit it to Jack, but she had started dancing with the girls, telling them it was time she taught them to dance. She bought a video of dance instructions and so far, they had practiced their technique on ballroom dancing, country line dancing, the two-step, even exotic dances like the tango. The girls got a kick out of it, but Maggie found it as educational for herself as for her daughters.

She relaxed in Jack's arms, drinking in the familiar scent of his cologne, letting herself revel in the touch of his hand against hers. His nearness overwhelmed her, her senses whirling to life. He leaned toward her, and she could feel his breath in her hair. This time she followed her earlier inclination and let her cheek rest against his chest. She could hear the thumping of his heart.

How did he feel about her? Except she sort of knew, didn't she? Hadn't he kissed her? She had been afraid to tell Billie about the kiss, afraid her friend would laugh, or lecture her about going after him. Maggie wasn't about to do that. If anything developed between them, it would have to happen naturally. She would not force it.

Too soon, the song ended and turned into a fast dance. Maggie had not had the nerve to do that with the girls. Jack let her go and drew back. Maggie stood unmoving, staring at him as he began to gyrate in time to the music, arms flying in different directions.

"I've never danced like that," she admitted, not certain what he expected her to do.

"You have good rhythm. Just move in time to the music." He demonstrated a move, and she laughed.

"You look like you've lost all your bones."

"Either that or my mind," he chortled. "Go ahead and try it. No one's going to tease you. Look at some of these guys. They're terrible dancers."

Maggie let him talk her into swaying in time to the music and before long she was laughing as she attempted new steps. The entire night took on a magical flavor. She found herself able to talk at the table with Virginia, Lydia and their husbands, much as she had on the computer. Every time she looked at Jack, a spark ignited inside her, and she could not stop smiling.

Later, Maggie was invited to dance by several of the men, but it was dancing in Jack's arms late in the evening that she really felt alive. More alive than she had ever felt as a woman. Her whole body was warm as it pressed to his. Her insides were filled with an aching want. She leaned toward him, burying her face against his chest, again hearing that thumping heart. She rubbed her cheek against his chest, and his breath caught.

"Jack?" she said, looking up at him. "Am I being too forward?"

He chuckled slightly and his fingers tapped at her nose. "Only you would ask that, Maggie."

"I guess. But I haven't been in any sort of relationship for a while. All this is new to me." She winced. Her words sounded like a cliché.

A dimple dented his cheek as he smiled down at her. "I know. Are you about ready to go?"

Maggie wanted to say no. She wanted the night to go on forever, but not many couples remained on the floor. The Garcias had already left and Lydia was waving goodbye from the door.

They drove home in companionable silence. Her house was nearly dark. The only light still on was by the computer. Billie was probably online.

"Would you like coffee?" he offered, glancing at the house as though thinking the same thing she was. If they went to her house, Billie would be there. Did he want to be alone with her?

"Sure," she said. He took her hand as they walked to his house and Maggie's heart began to throb. Her skin tingled with awareness. As they walked inside, he grasped her hand tighter. Night lights glowed in the gloomy interior and as he closed the door, he pulled her toward him.

Maggie nearly tripped, but then she was leaning against his hard chest, her nostrils inhaling the warm wonderful scent of him, her heart hammering against her chest. He released her hand and his arms wrapped around her, holding her body against his.

"Oh, Maggie," he whispered into her hair. "Maggie, Maggie, Maggie. Wonderful, magnificent Maggie."

Her name sounded glorious on his lips, and she looked up, her eyes stopping at the thin thatch of dark hair that sprouted from the open neck of his shirt. She'd always been fascinated with that hair, and her fingers touched it, outlining the neck of his shirt. As her eyes lifted she found his clear blue eyes filled with hot desire. It had been a long time since she had seen that look in a man's eyes. It felt good.

Maggie could feel the strength of his body against hers as he held her. Her breath quickened and for a second she feared he might let her go and head for the kitchen to make coffee, but just as she was wishing he would do it, he leaned down and dropped his lips to hers.

The kiss was filled with warmth, and her body tingled as his lips explored hers. She opened her eager mouth to him as her body trembled slightly.

Wrapping her arms around his shoulders, Maggie stood on her toes to meet his kiss forcefully. She had no idea what she was doing, but her lips seemed to have a will of their own, opening to his, seeking his, asking for more, responding in a way she didn't know she could.

His tongue snaked out, licking the edges of her lips and then darting inside as he deepened the kiss. Maggie moaned deep in her throat, her insides growing liquid and hot as molten lava. A pain grew deep in her lower regions and her heart raced.

She wanted him. She knew what that was now, to physically desire a man to the point of hurting as a way of proclaiming their love.

Love! No, this wasn't proclaiming love. This was what? Physical desire?

"Wait," she said, her breath coming in quick, uneven gasps.

"I'm sorry," he said. "I didn't mean to push anything."

"You're not. I don't want this to be because you feel sorry for me."

"Oh, Maggie," he groaned. "I don't feel sorry for you." He caught her hands and brought them to his lips.

In the dim light she could make out fiery lights in his eyes. The flames of desire! He wanted her as badly as she wanted him.

"I feel sorry for me," he said.

"For you?"

"Because you're so sweet, so wonderful, so beautiful."

No one had ever called her that before. Not even Al had ever spoken to her that way.

"Would you have even looked at me before I got rid of my glasses or lost weight?" she asked.

His chuckle was quick and he kissed her fingers again. "I did. I always thought you were sweet and your eyes were pretty, and your skin so soft. I like your new weight, but it never mattered. You used to call yourself pudgy old Maggie, but I never thought of it that way. I like a woman who looks like a woman, not one of these scarecrows."

"Your wife..." she began.

He put his fingers to her lips to stop her from saying more. "Billie said something to me tonight that made me think."

"Billie?"

"Yes. She made me realize what has been happening all along. I've been afraid of getting too involved with you because I might get hurt. But she asked tonight what I'd feel now if I lost you. And when I saw you dancing with those guys tonight... Well, maybe I wanted to set you up so I could leave, but now... now I know I can't do that. I don't want them to have you."

His words rattled around in her head. "Are you saying... you want me?"

"I don't know what I want. I guess..." He leaned over and kissed her quickly again. "I guess what I'm saying is remember when I said I wanted to take you out? Well, I think we move to the next step now. And see where we go from here."

Maggie's heart was pounding so hard she feared he could hear it. She'd never been so happy in all her life. And yet she wanted him to kiss her again, to resume those magical touches with his lips that brought fire to her veins. She clutched his hand and reached up and kissed him.

"Yes," she whispered against his lips. "Oh, yes."

Jack walked her home and strolled back across his front lawn again, aware that Maggie had not yet gone inside. He had a feeling she was composing herself, much as he needed to compose himself. The touch of her lips still sizzled on his.

What a magnificent night. Jack had not felt this good since... well, he didn't want to think that it was when Carla was alive. This was different.

Different and yet the same. As he had watched Maggie at the party, he'd discovered how strongly he felt about her. As he'd watched her dance with other men, the knowledge had come. He was falling in love with her. No, not falling. Already there. He'd watched her talking with them, smiling up at them, and realized he wanted those smiles exclusively for himself. He had no right to ask for them yet. That was what had made him think he should propose to her they move on to the next step.

He hopped up his steps, opened the door and walked inside. As he so often did when he walked into the house, Jack's eyes sought out Carla's picture. Maybe he should move it to another location. Not that he would ever forget her. But she was gone from his life. Her memories would live on, she would always be part of him. But his future was elsewhere. Perhaps the time had come to seek it out.

Maggie, his heart sang. Magnificent Maggie.

Twelve

"Say that again," Maggie said, sinking into the chair as though she was a deflating balloon. Jack's final, lingering kiss had left her insides buzzing.

Maggie had not wanted to explain the evening to Billie, and was prepared to plead a headache, anything but having to talk about what had just happened. Her whole body was alive, excited. She feared Billie would see her feelings, but what she walked into was worse than that.

The twins and Billie were seated around the computer and they greeted Maggie with startling news, news she could barely believe, news that tilted her world to a dizzying level she could only right by sitting down. She looked from one to the other, waiting to hear the words again.

"I found our dad," April repeated. May hovered next to her with wide, blue eyes filled with concern.

The words registered this time, like a bomb going off in her head. "Why would you try such a ridiculous thing?" Maggie asked.

"Why not? You've always said he would come back. We wanted him to know where we were."

"How... how... did you find him?"

"On the computer," April replied, pointing at the monitor.

"I thought I told you to give that up," Maggie said, fighting irritation, though it poured out in her strident voice.

"It seemed like a good idea," May said.

Maggie's temples throbbed with pain. The headache had been coming since April's announcement that they had found Al Williams. She rubbed her hands against her cheeks, putting them in front of her lips, her overly sensitive lips. Could they tell what she'd been doing over at Jack's house?

A sudden bout of disloyalty swept through her. Moments ago she'd been in another man's arms. But it had seemed so right!

"You had no right to do this." It wasn't fair! Just when things seemed ready to go in a good direction. Now this!

Billie rose to her feet. "Maybe I should go."

"No," Maggie said sharply, holding up her hand as though that might stop her. She fought anger. "Was this your idea?"

"It wasn't my doing, but I helped them. I'm sorry, Mag. I thought it was what you wanted. Has something changed?" Her eyes flashed sideways, toward Jack's house, though she said nothing. Maggie had a feeling Billie knew what was happening between her and Jack, though neither woman talked about it.

Maggie bit back her frustration. It wasn't Billie's fault; she had always said that. But she didn't know what she wanted. Waving her hands up and down to get air to her lungs, she battled to get a handle on her feelings. "This is just... shocking."

"Is there a reason you're afraid to see him, Mom?" May asked, ever the sharp twin, the one with the ability to sense something going on beneath the surface.

Maggie considered that. Was she afraid to see him? Or was it because of what she thought might be happening with Jack? There was no answer. Everything was so uncertain.

Jack had made a pledge to take the next step--whatever that was--but he would be gone in less than a month. He had brought back the cheer to her life, made her feel more like a woman than even Al had, but he had not said he loved her. In the meantime, the tightness in her chest, the need in her lower areas said Maggie was falling in love with him.

Now Al might be back. Why was she fighting the thought of seeing him again?

"Is it because of those guys?" Billie asked quietly. "Surely you're not still afraid of rejection?"

Maggie jerked her face to Billie, appalled she had brought up the rejection she'd suffered at the hands of Bob and Rich.

She'd never told the girls about Las Vegas.

"What guys?" April asked.

Maggie waved her hand at Billie and then inhaled sharply as she faced the girls. "Okay, I tried to meet someone from the computer when I went to Las Vegas. But if I hadn't won that jackpot, I would have come home a loser. Those guys were not interested in fat old mothers."

"You're no longer fat," May noted. "I thought you were changing 'cause you were hoping we might find him."

That idea shocked Maggie, and she shook her head. "That was never the point."

"Aren't you curious about him?" May prodded, getting to her feet and picking up a sheet of paper from the desk top.

"He's curious about us," April added. "He wants to see us."

"What?" Maggie's cry reverberated around the room. "You've already talked to him?"

"We talked to him tonight online," April admitted, coming toward her behind May.

Maggie whirled to Billie. "Did you know they were going to do this?"

Billie shook her head slowly, guilt visible in her eyes. "We've looked for him before, but didn't find him until tonight."

"He lives close by," May said in a quiet, calm voice as she approached Maggie. "In Jean, Nevada." She dropped a slip of paper on the arm of the chair.

Again, shock ripped through her as Maggie viewed the address scribbled on the paper. In her trips to Las Vegas, she had seen the sign for Jean. It was less than two hours away. To think, Al had been there all along.

"We didn't mean to upset you," April said, dropping onto the other arm next to Maggie. "But don't you think we have the right to know our dad?"

Maggie couldn't drag her eyes from the paper. "He hasn't been much of a dad. He's been close and never tried to see you."

The harsh words were as much of a surprise to her as they were to the girls. Only weeks ago she harbored thoughts of finding him herself. What had happened to her feelings for him?

So many questions, so few answers. She lurched to her feet. "I don't want to think about this right now. You need to get to bed, and maybe you should check on Kayla. She wasn't doing very well this morning. Maybe we need to take her to the vet."

The old sheepdog was showing severe signs of age, almost as though she were an extension of Maggie's feelings for Al.

"One thing," May said as the girls turned to the door and Billie got to her feet.

"What?" Maggie asked in exasperation.

"We told him we want to meet him. We gave him our address."

"Go check on Kayla," she ordered. "And then get to bed. We can talk more about this in the morning."

The girls exchanged looks of resignation. They would not protest further. They knew better than to argue with Maggie when she was angry, and right now frustration vibrated from her. Maggie wasn't even certain why.

Billie waited until the twins were outside and then walked over to Maggie. She rubbed Maggie's shoulder gently.

"What is it, hon? You don't want him back, do you?"

Maggie turned to look at her unhappily. "I don't know. I think... I may be falling in love with Jack..."

"Oh, my," Billie said breathlessly.

Maggie put her fist to her mouth. "I have no idea what I want. Jack isn't going to fall in love with me. I have to remember that. He'll be gone soon and I'll never see him again. Just like Al."

"Jack is not Al," Billie said softly.

Unhappily, she peered at Billie. Her friend was watching her with warm, concern-filled eyes. "I guess I have to see him again, don't I? No matter what? The girls are so vulnerable and they want to see their dad. It's not fair to keep him from them."

~ * ~

The pounding on Jack's door didn't wake him up. He'd already been out for his daily run. He felt great this morning, alive and filled with energy despite the growing heat. He could hardly wait for the moment he saw Maggie. He'd been watching her house to see if there was movement, but there had been none.

The lights had been on in the computer area when he had gone to bed the night before. Surely Maggie wasn't pursuing those men online anymore, was she? Then he thought of how luminous her eyes had been as they had danced, how they'd glittered in the night lights after they'd kissed. No, she would not be looking for someone else. He had seen the truth in her eyes. She wanted him as badly as he wanted her.

But was it only physical wanting? Or was there more? He couldn't imagine life without her around now, but what could it mean? Was he really in love with her? It wasn't like it had been with Carla, but he wouldn't expect it to be. This was different, but every bit as thrilling and he couldn't take the thought of losing her and the girls, just as Billie had said.

He knew he needed to take his time, for both their sakes. Her uncertainty and honesty had touched him the night before. Only Maggie would make such a painful declaration. He knew she had not been with anyone since Al. He could hardly wait to see her, to start showing her how special love could be.

The pounding was like an omen. Not everything was right.

May's pale face greeted him at the door.

"Kayla's dead," she said, tears welling in her blue eyes. "I checked on her last night, and she was okay, but now when I went out, she was... dead, I think."

Jack followed her out of the house, pulling on a shirt as he walked. He saw no sign of Maggie's car.

"Where's your mom?" he asked.

"She got called to work. I guess her boss was sick."

"Does she know?" He could imagine how hurt Maggie would be by the death of the old sheepdog.

"Not yet. I didn't know what to do."

He put his hand on her arm. "Don't worry. I'll take care of it, and I'll go tell her."

Relief crossed May's face. She wouldn't go near the dog as Jack walked over and touched Kayla's paw. The dog was stiff. It didn't take much to see that she was dead.

"She was just too old," May moaned. "And just when things were going to change."

Jack's head jerked up. "Change?"

Her tearful face lit up in a smile. "We found our dad."

"Al Williams?" The name slid from his lips like a whisper.

She nodded quickly, eagerly. "Yes, we found him last night. He's coming to see us."

His heart plunged. Al was back. Finally. After all these years, he would be coming to claim Maggie and her girls. A sick sadness overtook him.

"I'll take the dog to the vet," he offered. "He'll take care of her for you."

The next hour seemed to move in slow motion. He took the body to the only vet in Cactus Bluffs before driving to the store.

Sunday morning was usually quiet and this day was no exception. Later, travelers from Los Angeles would crowd the store as they made their journey home from weekends in Las Vegas, but right now it was empty.

Maggie was scrubbing the hotdog grill as he walked in. Her eyes refused to meet his, and Jack felt pain stab his insides. She was wearing her glasses today, and he noted her eyes were red rimmed. Did she already know about Kayla?

"Hi, Maggie," he said, stopping in front of the counter, shifting from one foot to another. He wanted to touch her, but he knew he didn't have the right. "I... Kayla is dead."

Her head jerked up and a cry escaped her. "No."

"May called me over a little while ago."

Maggie put down her cloth and came around the corner of the counter. Jack caught her as she suddenly sagged. She felt wonderful in his arms, but there was more than fire in his veins. As he helped her toward the snack bar area to sit down, he found his heart filling with more. He loved her. Maybe not the same as Carla, but he did love her.

Maggie's big brown eyes fastened on him. "What now?"

He explained what he had done and what her options were. She took it all in, her eyes staring straight ahead.

But there was more to the tension between them than just explaining Kayla's death. Finally she turned to him. She brushed her fingers against his wrist, a scorching touch and he couldn't help but take hold of her hand. He grasped it, and she squeezed his hand. Tears clouded her eyes.

"They found Al," she said, her eyes filled with misery.

He nodded curtly. "May told me."

She blinked, eyes avoiding his. "He wants to see us. To see them."

Again that pain stabbed into him, the pain he never wanted to feel again, the pain of loss. "You're going to see him?" he said, though it was more of a statement than a question.

"I have to," she said softly. Her eyes met his. She seemed to search his eyes for something, but he had no answers. He released her hand and stood up.

"I better get going. I promised one of the guys I'd help him paint his house."

A far away look grew in her eyes. She bit her lip as though considering something, then turned pleading eyes to him. "Will I see you later?"

Jack attempted a smile. "If you want."

"Yes." She caught his arm again. "And thanks for dealing with Kayla. I don't think I could have done that without you."

He wanted to say he would always be there for her, but a lump tightened in his throat. He only nodded instead.

~ * ~

Maggie dragged herself home, pleased that the day was finally over. She hadn't expected to be working, but in a way, it was a blessing. After a morning that dragged, the late afternoon had been very busy, keeping her from the many thoughts that tried to swirl around in her head.

Jack wanted to go in a new direction with their relationship, but she had not seen that in his face when he came to tell her about Kayla. Her trusted companion for so many years was gone. But Al was back. Or might be.

The girls had come by during the most crowded part of the morning, right after church when families were stopping for gas and snacks as they went home or headed out for picnics. She had not given them a chance to say anything, though she could tell they wanted to say more about Al.

The house was empty when she arrived, thankfully. Maggie collapsed on the sofa. A spring bit into her back. *Darn thing.* She needed to get new furniture. Maybe before Al came to see them.

Thoughts she'd had from time to time during the day raced back into her head. If Al was so close to Cactus Bluffs, why had he never come to see them? He should have known she would not leave. It was strange to think of him so near all this time and never attempting to see her or the girls.

The door burst open. The twins stood there together, their hair flying wildly about them in excitement.

"Mom, he's here!"

"What?" she cried, sitting straight up.

"That's what we were trying to tell you today. He said he might come and to watch for a blue Dodge truck. I think it just turned down the highway that leads into town."

Maggie began to shake. Could it be true? Was Al Williams returning? She peered out the window, wondering if the girls could be wrong. The truck was there. A blue Dodge Dakota had turned onto the lane that led to their driveway.

"Oh, my gosh," Maggie said, looking at the girls in horror.

"Go fix your hair, Mom," April said in an excited tone.

"And put on some make-up."

"We'll talk to him," May volunteered, her eyes looking concerned. "I hope he's as nice and easy to talk to as Jack."

Maggie didn't want to think about Jack right now. She started to direct the girls to dress up, and saw they had stayed in their Sunday best. She had thought they were going to a church function when they'd visited the store. Instead, they were anticipating Al's arrival. She had only herself to blame for this surprise. If only she'd listened instead of cutting short their explanations, she wouldn't have been caught unprepared.

The girls bounded out the door. Maggie peered through the Venetian blinds, watching as Al stepped from the truck.

He was as tall as she remembered, but the straw-blonde hair on his head was gone. Only a sandy fringe around the sides remained. His broad shoulders slumped and his firm body had given way to time. Too much food had given him a thick belly.

She stared at the man she had dreamed about for so many years. He wore jeans and a denim shirt that pulled tight across a thick middle.

Maggie looked down at her jeans and ran her fingers through her hair. Who was she kidding? She was who she was, and so was Al. Then she thought of Rich and Bob. Their condemning eyes came to her, and Maggie hurried into the bedroom.

She put on a new sundress she'd never worn, a pink dress with a bold display of colors that stood out against her light skin. She dabbed on foundation and rubbed rouge across her cheeks. Her hands were shaking so badly she didn't bother with eyeliner, though she did apply a light coating of blue eye shadow. Her eyes had hurt, so she'd taken off her contacts, and now her trembling hands prevented her from putting them back in.

A couple of strokes with the mascara brush, and she put on her thick glasses. She pinned up her hair, which was frizzy due to a day in the air-conditioned store. From the living room, she could hear laughing. The voice was familiar and sent a piercing through her heart. Al! Al was back.

The phone rang, and she grabbed it from her bedside table, expecting it to be Billie. The girls had probably told her he might be coming.

Jack's voice was a surprise, but it sent her heart to thumping. Was it guilt she felt?

"Maggie? I'm finishing up here. I wanted to see if maybe I should pick up some hamburgers and we can have a barbecue this evening. Maybe some ice cream for the girls?"

Tears clouded her eyes, and Maggie clutched the phone. Suddenly she didn't want to go into that other room. She didn't want to see Al and what he might mean. She wanted to stay in the dim shadows and talk to Jack. Maybe they might argue, but in the end they would laugh. Most of all, she wanted to touch him, to have him touch her, to see the light of desire flare in his eyes.

Her breath came out in a rush. "Al's here," she said. "Maybe... maybe another time?"

His disappointment was audible. "Sure. Another time."

Maggie stared at herself in the mirror. The woman who faced her was so different from the woman who had gone to Las Vegas to meet Bob. She finished her ensemble with dangling earrings and went down the hall to see Al.

He slouched on the worn chair, shifting from side to side, looking decidedly uncomfortable. The girls sat on the sofa, across from him, chattering away. Maggie met his eyes as she came into the room. She gave him a hesitant smile. The bright eyes had faded to a dull blue, but his smile was still quick.

The crooked smile that had once melted her heart did nothing. This was not the Al she remembered. Or maybe her memories had been faulty, born of teenage dreams. Maggie stepped forward to greet the stranger as her dreams from the past vanished.

He nodded toward her. "Hello, Maggie," he said.

"You've met the twins," she said, smiling happily at them. Actually she was pleased that he evoked no sense of excitement in her. What if he'd been the handsome man she pictured in her mind? What would she have felt then?

As he spoke in the voice that had not changed, she realized she would have felt little. She met his eyes. Was that disappointment she saw?

"It's good to see you," she said, keeping her voice as pleasant as possible.

"We'll get the iced tea," May said, hopping to her feet. She grabbed April's arm when her sister didn't move. April started to protest, but May yanked her to her feet with a warning look.

Maggie sat on the sofa across from Al. His gaze wandered around the room as though he was looking for something in particular, and she could almost see the distaste in them.

"The girls are full of energy," he said, crossing one leg over his knee and shaking it.

"They have been since they were born," she replied. Maggie had no idea what to say. It was like talking to a stranger. "Did they tell you Kayla died this morning?"

"Kayla?" He shook his head, uncertainty written in his eyes.

"Your dog? The one you left with me?"

He leaned his head back and slowly a smile came to him. "Oh, yeah, that old mutt. I'd forgotten about her."

Maggie felt tears, for Kayla's loss and for herself. She had always thought that Al might come back, at least for the dog. How many things had she deluded herself about him?

He cleared his throat, looking toward the kitchen. "Well, you seem to have done okay with them."

"I guess. It's been rough at times."

He studied his dusty boots. "I was surprised you had them look for me."

Maggie drew back. "You think I had them look for you?"

His eyes wandered around the small interior. "Well, I can see you need help. I can try to give it, if you want. But I got a couple of kids of my own. And I just got divorced. Not that I'm free, you know. I got a gal, and we been talking marriage."

Anger burst into Maggie's chest. "Do you think I had them find you to get you back? To help us out?"

His look of condescension sent anger piercing through her. "Didn't you? I mean, you ain't married, right? They made it sound like you've been pining away for me all this time. No other guys wanted to take up with you 'cause you'd put on weight."

She pressed her lips together wanting to attack him, to unload all the pain she'd felt in the past thirteen years, the longing she'd felt, but it didn't come. His words of rejection couldn't hurt her any worse than realizing she'd been waiting for a false dream that was never coming true.

The twins burst through the door carrying a tray with a big pitcher of lemonade, interrupting them. Maggie sat back on the sofa, letting the girls carry the conversation. There was little more she had to say to Al. Let him think she wanted him back. It didn't matter. And neither did he. The twins could see him if they wanted from time to time, but she doubted she would ever see him again.

~ * ~

Darkness shrouded the walkway as Maggie stepped toward Jack's house. Maybe she was being forward. Maybe she would face another rejection. Her heart pounded, her nerves screeched, because she knew this rejection would matter.

Al's words had not hurt her, but she would never sleep tonight if she couldn't find out what might be ahead with Jack.

She tapped at his door and when he answered, Maggie held out the plate of cookies she'd baked. Al's visit had left her in a strange mood, and when the girls had gone to tell their friends about meeting their father, she'd spent the evening in a frenzy, baking cookies, a cake, even two pies, despite the sweltering heat.

Jack drew back and then a wide smile crossed his face. He pulled open the door wider. "Maggie! What a great surprise."

"I was trying some of the recipes you left with the girls," she said, hoping he was being honest. "Take them before I drop them." She tried to make her words teasing, but the truth was her shaking hands were unsteady.

He took the plate and beckoned her inside. The coolness of his house was refreshing after her hot kitchen.

Maggie stood in the middle of the room in her pink sun dress, wondering if she should have come. Billie had suggested it, but maybe her friend had been wrong. Look how she had been hurt when she'd sought out those guys in Las Vegas. Look at how Al had rejected her. And while she'd fixed her face again, she still couldn't wear her contacts.

She pushed her glasses up her nose.

"Sit down," Jack offered, pointing to the sofa.

Maggie perched on the edge and he sat beside her. In a t-shirt and jeans, he had never looked more appealing. She wanted to touch him, but held back, fearing his response. He hadn't sounded pleased when he'd heard about Al visiting.

His blue eyes watched her, a frown crossing his face. "Maggie, I have to know. How did it go with Al?"

She should have known he would be curious. She'd already been through this with Billie. This was far worse though. Tears clouded her eyes as she shook her head.

"Awful. All those years I waited." She pressed her hands to her eyes. "I'm sorry. I didn't want to get emotional."

"Go ahead." His sudden chuckle was a surprise.

"It wasn't funny," she said, dropping her hands to her lap. Was he going to lecture her about this, as he had about the two computer men? Maggie didn't think she could take that.

He held out hand toward her, then pulled it back, as though afraid to touch her. "I'm sure it wasn't. I'm just pleased."

"Pleased?" she questioned. "Why would you be pleased?"

He shook his head. "Sorry. Go on. What happened?"

She drew an unsteady breath. Jack had been such a good friend, but now he was acting funny, too. Why was he pleased? But that could wait. She need to tell him about Al.

"He was a jerk. He thought I wanted money from him and that I was going to try to force myself on him because no one would ever want me." She thought of Al's condemning eyes. If Jack did the same, she didn't know what she'd do.

His tongue ran over his lips and she realized his breath was coming quickly.

"He was wrong. Remember what I said last night. I want us to be together, Maggie. I want you. You have no idea how frightened I was by his coming back. How I fantasized all day that you'd tell me you were going away with him."

His sincerity made him sound like a hurt boy, and Maggie's fears vanished. She touched his hand. As usual, excitement coursed through her.

"No. He didn't want me, and I don't love Al. Not anymore. I'm not sure I ever did. I was a little girl back then. I didn't even know what love was. Maybe that's why it doesn't hurt so much to lose that dream."

His smile widened and he turned his hand over and clasped hers, squeezing it. "And you think you know what love is now?"

The knowledge flowed through her like a warm river of water, and then stopped, dammed up by a flood of new emotions. Tears flooded her eyes again, and she nodded. She drew her hand free of his, and spoke through the lump that was forming in her throat, one that promised a lifetime of pain.

"But you know what? I just realized something. I can't go through that again. I love you, Jack, and I know you're leaving next month. I can't move to that next level, or whatever it was you wanted. I can't. 'Cause I couldn't spend the rest of my life waiting here, thinking you might come back."

He took her hand back, shaking his hand. "Oh, Maggie, I can't leave without you. Do you want to go to New Mexico?"

She swallowed hard as the words soaked into her muddled brain. "You're... You want me to go with you?"

His smile was sweet and filled with love. "You and the girls. I love you all too much to leave you behind."

Maggie didn't know what to say. She started to ask about his wife and then as her gaze swung toward the other room, she realized the picture was gone from his desk. Turning back toward Jack, she nodded. "I can't think of anything I'd rather do."

He leaned toward her and kissed her softly, his lips gentle and searching. As he moved forward, Maggie pulled back to remove her glasses.

"These things, they're always in the way."

"I love you with them or without them. And so you know, I love the new Maggie, but it was the old one who won my heart."

Her heart swelled with pleasure, and she couldn't reply.

"I'm sorry you waited so long for Al, only to find out he wasn't the right person."

"I'm not sorry I waited," she replied, brushing her fingers across his cheek. "I was waiting for the right man. And just like I always dreamed, he did come."

Meet *Rebecca Grace*

Rebecca Grace is the pen name for Rebecca Martinez, an award winning former broadcast journalist who is now writing fiction. This is her second romance novel for Wings Press. Her romance LOVE ON DECK was released in July and her next romance HOME FIRES BURNING will be released in 2005. Currently she lives in Aurora, Co where she works in public relations and is writing her next novel. For more information, please visit her website at www.rebeccagrace.com

Letter to Our Readers

Enjoy this book?

You can make a difference

As an independent publisher, Wings ePress, Inc. does not have the financial clout of the large New York Publishers. We can't afford large magazine spreads or subway posters to tell people about our quality books.

But, we do have something much more effective and powerful than ads. We have a large base of loyal readers.

Honest Reviews help bring the attention of new readers to our books.

If you enjoyed this book, we would appreciate it if you would spend a few minutes posting a review on the site where you purchased this book or on the Wings ePress, Inc. webpages at: https://wingsepress.com/